I0524472

THE DEVIL IN A DOMINO

"CHAS. L'EPINE"

THE DEVIL IN A DOMINO

A REALISTIC STUDY

With a new introduction by
SIMON STERN

VALANCOURT BOOKS

Originally published by Lawrence Greening & Co., London, 1897
First Valancourt Books edition 2017

This edition © 2017 by Valancourt Books
Introduction and notes © 2017 by Simon Stern

Published by Valancourt Books, Richmond, Virginia
http://www.valancourtbooks.com

All rights reserved. The use of any copyrighted part of this
publication reproduced, transmitted in any form or by any means,
electronic, mechanical, photocopying, recording, or otherwise, or
stored in a retrieval system, without prior written consent of the
publisher, constitutes an infringement of the copyright law.

All Valancourt Books publications are printed on acid free paper
that meets all ANSI standards for archival quality paper.

Cover: A reproduction of the original cover art of the 1897 edition,
colorized by M. S. Corley, to whom the Publishers are grateful for
his assistance.

ISBN 978-1-943910-82-3 (hardcover)
ISBN 978-1-943910-83-0 (paperback)
Also available as an electronic book.

Set in Dante MT

INTRODUCTION

When it first appeared, in 1897, *The Devil in a Domino* provoked some reviewers to disgust and others to admiration. The *Edinburgh Evening News* found it "a peculiarly repulsive piece of writing, indicative of the low and morbid type of so-called literature which is purveyed to a half-educated constituency," and suggested that it might furnish a useful exhibit for "coroners who ... make severe remarks about message boys' pernicious reading." For this reviewer, a novel that claimed to explore the causes of crime was more likely to worsen the problem than to aid in its understanding. More bluntly, *The Academy Fiction Supplement* declared that if the author was seeking to "exemplify the most awful workings of heredity," he had succeeded "only by means too crude for art and too horrible for enjoyment"; while *The Literary World* called the book "a frankly horrible performance ... a gruesome compound of madness and butchery," which "no sane person could find pleasure in reading." On the other hand, the *Hampshire Telegraph* described the novel as "exceedingly creepy," and commended the author for "handling a gruesome subject in as delicate a manner as possible," the Dundee *Evening Telegraph* predicted that the story's "diabolical horrors" would satisfy "those who like to sup on sensation," and the *North British Advertiser* found the novel unputdownable: "Altogether the book, like the ideal ghost story, proves so fascinating that once it is started the very fear it awakes impels one to read it on to the end." The London *Star* went even further, commending the novel in language that must have gladdened the author and publisher alike: "May be guaranteed to disturb your night's rest. It is a gruesome, ghastly, blood-curdling, hair-erecting, sleep-murdering piece of work, with a thrill on every page. Read it."

Such a disparate set of reactions among the reviewers is bound to pique a reader's curiosity, and in this case, the reason for these contrasting views is not far to seek. The novel blends a peculiar kind of deadpan humor with elements from sensation fiction, the gothic, and late-nineteenth-century degeneration theory, all organized in a narrative loosely based on the Ripper murders of a decade earlier. Aleck Severn, the main character, recalls by turns the split-personality protagonist of Stevenson's *The Strange Case of Dr. Jekyll and Mr. Hyde* (1886) and such reclusive, introspective aesthetes of decadent fiction as des Esseintes in Huysmans's *Against Nature* (1884), while the novel is generally suffused with the sort of weird and eerie ambience that pervades Bram Stoker's *Dracula* (1897) and Richard Marsh's *The Beetle* (1897). As this description suggests, the novel also owes something to *The Picture of Dorian Gray* (1890/91). Indeed, Wilde makes a notable appearance in Max Nordau's *fin-de-siècle* treatise on the ills afflicting modern civilization (translated into English in 1895 as *Degeneration*), and hereditary exhaustion figures among the factors responsible for the social collapse that Nordau diagnoses; L'Epine's novel, in its treatment of heredity, reads like a transposition of Nordau's theories into fiction.

The Devil in a Domino begins with a matter-of-fact summation of Severn's birth, the result of a marriage between an aristocratic "profligate and ... scoundrel" and a "drunkard" who dances at fairs but managed to be "sober at the wedding." She has already killed her husband before the end of the first page, and the novel quickly turns to the questions about "hereditary taint" that drive much of the plot. Is Severn cursed from birth, or will he be able to "expunge the stains left ... by his parents"? The title, of course, gives away the answer, and within a few pages Sev-

ern's withdrawal from society to a "lonely part of a northern suburb" suggests that he has already arrived at the first
stage of a career that will lead "straight [to] a madhouse, or
a grave," as one of his friends predicts. At this point, rather
surprisingly, Marianne Talbot persuades Severn to marry
her, but he quickly returns to his reclusive ways, only to
announce, after months of meditation, that he has solved
the problem which has been consuming him, and that he
is ready at last to enter society and to entertain on the scale
that his friends have expected. Thus far we have arrived at
the end of the book's first chapter, and I will disclose no
more of the plot except for a few details that will help to
situate the novel's literary genealogy.

Although the novel is presented as a fictionalized
account of the Ripper murders (a point that nearly every
reviewer noted), the plot does not follow the Whitechapel
killings very closely. Severn is responsible for only two murders, rather than the five now ascribed to Jack the Ripper,
let alone the eleven ascribed to him at the time; moreover,
Severn's method of cultivating a friendship with his victims
makes him very unlike Jack the Ripper. More accurately,
the novel might be described as an effort to explore the
psychology of a murderer in a way that combines Nordau's
theories of degeneration with the approach that Robert
Louis Stevenson takes in *Dr. Jekyll and Mr. Hyde*. Stevenson's
novella, published shortly before the Ripper killings, opens
with an assault and later describes a murder; L'Epine's
pacing follows this model, describing the first murder early
in the narrative, with a second one about half way through.
Just as Dr. Jekyll discovers a chemical process that will
allow him to explore the biological foundations of human
nature, Severn is obsessed with the puzzle of existence,
a puzzle expressed in pseudo-scientific terms: "The first
movement is life. But is it? What is *movement*? A toad lives
motionless a thousand years, an infant is stillborn: where

is the *vital* difference in the process of *their* production?"
Severn's solution, unlike Jekyll's, is physical, not chemical:
he is compelled to dissect women's bodies in search of the
answers to these questions. Whereas Stevenson structures
his narrative like a mystery, leaving us uncertain of the relationship between Jekyll and Hyde, L'Epine reveals at the
outset that Severn is leading a double life, as a man about
town known for "lavish hospitality and *bonhomie*" and a
deranged criminal responsible for the death of a woman
found "on the doorstep of a low lodging house in one
of the worst localities of the East End." Again, whereas
Stevenson does not reveal the nature of Dr. Jekyll's quest
until the story's close, in this case we are told, even before
the first death, what drives Severn to commit murder. The
narrative is, accordingly, fashioned on different lines from
Stevenson's, guided not by the question of how to explain
the horrific acts that punctuate the plot, but by the question of Severn's ultimate fate: how long will his career in
crime continue, and will he manage to escape justice?

As noted above, *Dorian Gray* also lurks in the novel's
background. Although we are not actually told that Severn
remains unchanged in the course of his exploits, there is
a strong implication that he transposes the ageing process
onto his assistant, Jem Pate, who appears prematurely
"bent and bowed as if with age, the face thin and lined,
and surmounted by locks of grayish hair, the eyes bleared
and dim." Marianne (and Severn's female victims) might
be regarded as the perfect exemplification of the fictional
heroine who is, in Eve Sedgwick's classic formulation,
"between men" in the sense that she functions to medi-
ate the vectors of a sort of desire that the male characters
cannot express directly to each other. For instance, when
she starts to realize how much time Severn is spending with
Jem Pate, Marianne becomes "jealous of that pale youth ...
on whom her husband looked ... with such strange affec-

tion." Both by acting (if only by implication) as the kind of surrogate that Dorian Gray finds in his painting, and by serving as the source for a muted homoerotic current that flickers through the course of the plot, the figure of Jem Pate hints at the story's roots in Wilde's novel, another tale of degeneration, cursed heredity, and split personality.

We may never be able to establish the author's identity. On the title page of the original edition, he is styled as "Chas. L'Epine," with the name enclosed in quotation marks. Greening published another novel attributed to L'Epine in 1899 (a werewolf tale called *The Lady of the Leopard*), and announced a few other forthcoming titles by him that did not appear; after that, we find no further trace of him. Douglas Anderson has argued persuasively that L'Epine's style and thematic interests resemble those of another writer whom Greening was then just starting to publish—C. Ranger Gull.[1] Some of Gull's early books appeared under the pseudonym Guy Thorne ("thorn" being, as Anderson observes, the English translation of the French *épine*), and the chronology of these publications might be taken to indicate that Gull began writing under the name of L'Epine and moved on to Thorne. Gull's novels *The Hypocrite* and *Miss Malevolent* were published anonymously by Greening in 1898 and 1899 respectively; Gull wrote *The Cigarette Smoker* under his own name in 1901; and first used the pseudonym Guy Thorne in 1902 for his novel *The Oven*, and again the next year for his bestselling tale *When It Was Dark*. (David Wilkinson, in his 2012 biography of Gull,[2] does not refer to L'Epine's writing, but Anderson had not yet published his essay on L'Epine at that time.) Both *The Hypocrite* and *Miss Malevolent* reflect

1 Douglas A. Anderson, "Late Reviews," *Wormwood* 23 (Autumn 2014), 75-78.
2 David Wilkinson, *'Guy Thorne': C. Ranger Gull: Edwardian Tabloid Novelist and His Unseemly Brotherhood* (Rivendale Press, 2012.)

Wilde's influence, as Angela Kingston has observed,[3] and Gull would later write (under the pseudonym Leonard Cresswell Ingleby) two biographical works on Wilde. None of this, of course, provides definitive proof of Anderson's theory, but Gull is so far the only likely possibility whom anyone has proposed. Perhaps future research will substantiate this hypothesis or will yield a better candidate.

Whoever the author was, *The Devil in a Domino* deserves to be better known. It was among the first novels to weave the events of the Ripper murders into its plot. Moreover, it is a fascinating and unholy combination of late-nineteenth-century social theories and literary genres, presented in a style that veers from the comic to the sensational. After its initial appearance, the novel was successful enough to warrant a reprint in a "cheap edition" in 1902. There are only a handful of copies of either edition still in existence, and we are grateful to Allison Kane and Louis Sherwood, in the Special Collections Department of the Texas Wesleyan University Library, for permitting the loan of their copy.

SIMON STERN
July 2017

SIMON STERN received his Ph.D. in English literature from Berkeley and his J.D. from Yale and is an associate professor at the University of Toronto, where he is a member of the Faculty of Law and the Department of English.

3 Angela Kingston, *Oscar Wilde as a Character in Victorian Fiction* (Palgrave Macmillan, 2007), 270-285

THE DEVIL IN A DOMINO.

CHAPTER I.

ALECK SEVERN'S father was gently born; he was also a profligate and a scoundrel. His mother was a drunkard. This was a pity, as she had her fine physical points, and was sober at the wedding. By profession, the wench danced at fairs, on the platform of the travelling booth, and did it better drunk than sober. But her gentleman husband drove her mad, and by the time she had to give up the dancing and the booth, her face used to purple at sight of him.

Then they began to look at one another to see which of them it was to be, and at last, in less than a twelve-month, she ended it, and in a drunken brawl, slipped a knife up to the haft into his heart.

A month later the accursed off-spring of their union was born, opening his eyes on prison walls to the shrieking sound of his dying mother's curse.

Priest and Levite passed the infant by, and, when afar off, strained careless eyes, hoping to see him dead, but the Gentle Samaritan came in time, and was not frightened by death-bed curses nor the threat of Heredity. She was of the father's race, and had wealth, an honourable name, and a peaceful home, to which, weeping tears of angelic pity, she carried the unconscious boy.

And thus, spite of birth, Aleck Severn was reared in a gentle, domestic atmosphere, educated in refinement, and equipped generally for a start in life with all those advantages for mind and body that are usually the prerogative of an only and well-loved son of mutually agreed and pious parents. Still the chances of hereditary taint were too great to be overlooked, and Aleck's advancing years were watched with morbid curiosity by those whose care he was and who knew his history. But, as the docile child grew into the studious youth and the youth into the sedate and attractive man, dubious relations began to draw sighs of relief, and to express the conviction that Aleck would yet bring sufficient honour to the family name to expunge the stains left on it by his parents. Some, indeed, whose execration of the wretched pair even their death could not assuage, felt ill-concealed disappointment that the offspring of their union showed no likelihood of affording expiation. "The curse is in his veins; he will hand it down to all time," they said. "Let him hang, and purge the family once and for all."

But these pessimists were few and far between and obtained small hearing, and when, at the age of six-and-twenty, Aleck was left sole inheritor of the very comfortable fortune owned by the paternal aunt who had adopted him, hearty congratulations met him on all sides from a large circle of personally-attached friends, among whom a few jealous croakers went for nothing.

At this time young Severn was tall and well-developed, with a dignity of bearing beyond his years; his face, surmounted by waving nut-brown hair, wore an habitual expression of gentle melancholy; the eyes were deep-set, and of a nice hazel colour, with handsome black lashes; the nose was large, and showed intelligence and power, while the mouth, firm, yet withal sweet as to the lips, had, at times, a certain pathetic droop about the corners, such as one sees in grieved or tired children. The idea of either beard or moustaches was abhorrent to him; some envious detractors, who had not a classical outline to hide, declared he could not grow either. Possibly so; hair of any description would have seemed as out of place on the pure clearness of Aleck Severn's skin and the almost womanly contour of his face, as on a god's head in marble.

For the, rest he was an accomplished gentleman, a good boon companion, spite of his quiet looks, and a favourite with the women, who, nevertheless, respected him. He was, moreover, a fair scholar and—this known only to himself—a deep and secretive thinker.

Reared in full expectation of the fortune he ultimately possessed, Severn had been educated for no one profession, nor had his studies ever been induced to take any particular bent. His aunt—always more or less superstitious concerning her charge—had once secretly carried him to a famous reader of character and professor of "bumps."

The solemn, melancholy-looking child seemed to attract the professor (who knew nothing of its history) a good deal.

"You say his bread is not only cut, but buttered for him to the end of the chapter?" said the psychologist, smoothly rubbing his hands; "well, that is a pity, for manual labour would be good for him. However, don't feed his imagination, he may be a 'one-idea'd' man, and such are better without too much for the one maggot to grub on; give his mind plenty of scope and he may turn out a lucky inventor, or astonish the world with a new scientific toy."

The good lady was much impressed with these sounding prognostications, and acted in the best way she could upon her own secret interpretation of them. Aleck's studies were desultory and wide, but all matter-of-fact, and his naturally romantic disposition was turned into the hard and fast groove of materialistic pursuits. Even as a boy young Severn was of opinion that to science—and thought—all things were possible, and as he grew older he took more and more to both, till, when at last complete master of himself, and his mind, and his money, thought, that for many years had walked hand-in-hand with knowledge, now outstripped it, and ran riot in regions which no philosopher has yet explored. "Severn will spoil himself," said his friends, "he broods too much." The little professor of "bumps" had not counselled wisely; that solemn, melancholy-looking child would have fared much better left to his imagination than to the dangerous devices of untrammelled scientific thought.

For about a year after his aunt's death, Severn spent his time much as other soberly-inclined young men similarly placed. He travelled at home and abroad, in company or alone, accepted others' hospitality and tendered it lavishly himself, and after a little money, and less time, expended in "seeing life" generally, made for himself a certain sort of reputation among *dilettanti,* who interested themselves in abstruse or heterodox pursuits. But just when admirers and friends were predicting with security that Aleck Severn's name was made, and that before him stretched a useful and brilliant career, about to be inaugurated by a most auspicious marriage, there came a sudden change, and the circle in which the young man had moved with such self-government and signal success knew him no more.

He abandoned his fashionable quarters in town, refusing any explanation, or declaring there was none to give, except it was found in the fact that he was sick of a trivial life in a trivial world. Deaf to expostulations, or more tender entreaty, he purchased a small house with extensive grounds in a lonely part of a northern suburb, and, taking but a week to make up his mind, retired there alone, assuming at once so entirely the ways and habits of a recluse that friends and acquaintances speedily grew weary of taking a tiring journey simply to be refused or told they were not wanted. So the hermit was left more and more to himself.

Some, with ominous shakes and frowns, declared that

here was the old taint creeping out at last; others opined that Severn had withdrawn himself to complete some startling scientific work that would make him famous; others, again, that the fad would speedily "burst up" in a reaction of dissipation: a few hinted at romantic suffering; one or two at miserliness, solitary drinking, vivisection, and any other more or less uncanny reason why a young man should isolate himself from his fellows; but most were agreed that Aleck Severn was of too gentle and melancholy a mould to have any unhallowed motives in his conduct. "He is simply eccentric, and he thinks too much;" this was the final verdict; and after the loss of his hospitable roof and board had been sufficiently deplored, his name ceased to occupy conversation, and interest in him died away to casual and careless mention.

But there was one heart that did not forget, and one to whom Aleck Severn's absence from his accustomed haunts day by day and month by month, summed up the whole difference between joy and misery.

Marianne Talbot was a girl of unusual worth and beauty, and owned the disposal of a considerable fortune as well as of her most lovely person, without let or hindrance. Her connections, moreover, were wealthy and influential, and when it was first noticed how sweetly she favoured the timid advances Aleck Severn had seemed to make when mingling in the society in which she moved, people had quoted him as too lucky a devil altogether, for if such as Marianne Talbot became mother to his children, heredity might well be exorcised. But Aleck's uncertain advances never developed into anything more, and so well did Marianne bear herself, that no one guessed her heartache when the man suddenly disappeared, like a frightened St. Antony to his cell, without even a pressure of the hand to show that the love she had not been able altogether to conceal, would not be forgotten or ignored.

At first the girl buoyed herself up easily enough: remonstrances and entreaties must prevail, and Aleck soon be with them again; then, as each hope proved delusive, pride sustained her. But, as time passed on, and all that she could hear of Severn was the strange tale of his complete isolation and increasing hatred of interruption, even pride failed her, and her misery found vent in a burst of woe and words.

Happily for her the friend in whom she confided was a brisk and bustling, kind-hearted little matron, who had no nonsense about her, and could not stand it in others. "You'll excuse me, dear," she said, when the burst was over, "but this only confirms me in my opinion that Aleck Severn is a fool. However, a certain percentage of fools is necessary, or wise men would never speak, and, if you'll take my advice, I think we can manage the young man yet."

Marianne smiled at this, and then wept afresh.

"Do not think," she sobbed, "that I would degrade myself by confessing to a love for a man who did not care for me; but he does care—have I not met his gaze, heard his tone, felt his touch?—I know that he loves me, only——"

"—Only he does not know it himself," broke in the matron briskly. "No, don't be offended; I quite understand, my dear; everyone thought there was going to be something between you, and if you had not been so proud and so plucky the young man would not have got off so easily. Of course he loves you, and equally, of course, he doesn't know it."

"Then what am I to do?" cried Marianne, "Heaven help me, I cannot live without him."

Women are born conspirators. Marianne's friend was sincerely sorry for her troubles, but her glory was in the chance of being able to conspire against the peace of the aggravating recluse, from whose garden door her own irreproachable Victoria had been more than once turned

ignominiously away. Marianne herself, having once con-
fessed her weakness, was entirely at her mercy, and was
gradually led to believe that the daring plan the brisk little
woman was not slow to propose, would not only end in
happiness for herself, but eventually rescue the man she
loved from the disastrous effects of a useless and selfish
seclusion.

"Your duty is plain enough," the matron would say, with
easy conviction. "There is Severn with everything that life
can offer, thinking himself to death in that out of the way
hole, and here are you, moping yourself into a shadow. Go
to him, open his eyes to a few plain facts, and then bless me
for the result."

Madame was quite carried away by her own scheme;
she hugged herself with the idea of being the means of
bringing Severn back to his world, and congratulated
herself on the footing she could claim in Marianne's future
establishment; this quite apart from her sympathy with
the girl, whom she was unconventional enough to have
advised according to the Golden Rule so neglected among
women. Still a full year passed away before her eloquent
persuasion, or the girl's own heartache, bore its fruit. Then
the chance words of a friend laid the last straw on her deci-
sion, and love and pity finally weighed down fear.

"I'm afraid Severn's case is hopeless," said this unconscious instrument of fate. "I managed to see him the other
day by waiting an hour or two, but he seems just as set in
his purpose as when he took it up. It seems a pity, too, that
there is no one to save him from himself; he's working
straight for a madhouse, or a grave."

" 'My dear fellow,' I said to him, 'what on earth do you
do with yourself here? There are no signs that you even
read.' He looked at me with his great, melancholy eyes, 'I
think,' he said. Think! My belief is that his parents' story
is rankling in his brain; he's not half the man he was, even

to look at, and if someone isn't soon found to take his case to heart, he'll pass out of existence in about as miserable a way as he came into it."

All this, spoken with good-natured unconcern, and to no one in particular, sank with burning force into Marianne's heart, and after a night of fierce self-conflict, without confiding her plan to anyone, she set out on foot, and alone, for the northern suburb. If the reminder of her love could recall Aleck Severn to a happier life, such offer of salvation should not be withheld.

The autumn sunshine was falling with melancholy beauty on the yellowing leaves in the closely walled-in garden as Marianne timidly rang for admission to the isolated home. The distant peal of the bell re-echoed through the stillness and caused her heart to beat nervously. She started at even the faint rustle of the plane leaves as they fluttered past her to the ground. The place was strangely lonely and deserted, and only the ugly lamp-posts, an occasional sight of an enterprising cab, and the still rarer glimpse of a policeman, convinced the wanderer that he was still within the metropolitan area, while the rattle of a tradesman's cart, the cheery call of a baker boy, or the shout of children, turned out to play in the deserted building plots, were the only signs of life.

Marianne's heart sank low as she waited, and she desperately wished that she had not come alone. The bright loneliness of the place grew so oppressive at last that she was about to forego her errand and beat a retreat, when the garden door unexpectedly opened and the kind voice of an elderly dame respectfully asked her what she wanted.

Vastly reassured by the woman's appearance, Miss Talbot handed her her card, on which she had pencilled a few lines, adding that she would remain where she was to await an answer from Mr. Severn.

"You had better step inside, ma'am," said the woman,

"I may be gone some time, and you will be glad of this garden seat."

After a moment's hesitation, Marianne entered the enclosure, the door was shut, and the dame was soon lost to view down the winding path. In after days Marianne recalled with many a pang that lost opportunity, when a few steps taken back into the open road would have saved her from the horrors that in time to come were to crush her into an unhallowed grave; but then her heart thrilled only with angelic thoughts of self-devotion. Five, ten, fifteen minutes passed, and Marianne had time to notice the beautiful order of the place, the neatly brushed paths, the handsomely stocked flower-beds, and the smooth lawn; this scarcely seemed to tally with the habits of a morbid recluse, and the girl agitated herself afresh as to the view Severn might take of her visit. Another intolerable quarter of an hour passed, and then the old dame came quietly into sight and beckoned her to approach.

"Mr. Severn will see you in the front garden, Miss," she said. "I am very sorry to have kept you waiting, but I had great difficulty in rousing him to look at your card, and even now I think he scarcely knows who you are."

This was not exactly a good beginning, but the woman herself seemed so pleasant and cheery that Marianne's fears subsided, and her heart leapt high at the nearness of the man she loved.

"This scarcely looks like the abode of one who lives so lonely a life," she said, as her guide led her through the wide hall of the Villa, where evidences of refinement and care were visible on every side.

"Oh, the master is very particular," the woman answered with her pleasant smile. "I have no one to help me, but he keeps things in order himself, and the garden is his particular care; he tends it every day. There is Mr. Severn, Miss; I will leave you now."

Aleck was seated on a rustic chair underneath a weeping ash, half-bared in places by the autumn winds. The trembling girl's first impression was that he was little changed; the face might be a trifle thinner and paler, and the broad shoulders have acquired a little stoop, but it was the same look as of old that was turned upon her as she advanced, and the same radiant smile that greeted her as she stretched out her hand.

At the sight, all the long pent-up love and yearning burst out in one wild cry.

"Oh, my dear, at last! Say that you have not forgotten and will forgive. You are killing yourself, they tell me. I could not keep away."

For a moment the man stood as if dazed, passing his hand across his eyes, then, as she flung herself at his knees on the grass, while she poured forth love, entreaty and reproach, he stooped lower and lower till he had at length gathered her in his arms, and so, after a moment, to his breast.

"Marianne," he whispered, "I have thought of many things, but never of this."

"Then think of it now," she cried, "and then *think* no more, but live; I have waited so long, Aleck! Come with me and be happy."

And the placid sunshine shone on an unusual sight in the "thinker's" lonely garden that afternoon.

* * * * * * * * * * *

When a few months later the news leaked out that Aleck Severn was married, had married secretly, and married, moreover, none other than the wealthy and beautiful Marianne Talbot, all the old interest was momentarily revived, and speculation ran high as to how the match had been brought about, and as to how and where the married

pair would settle when they returned from their conti-
nental trip. The idea that Severn, with so much money
and such a wife, would recommence his old thinking
ways, scarcely occurred to the most lugubrious friends,
and acquaintances rubbed up their tarnished interest and
rehearsed the chaff that was to be Severn's portion for the
good use he had made of his retirement. But loud was the
wonder and disgust when it became known that Aleck
and his wife had come back indeed, but *not* to inaugurate
a new state of things. Mrs. Severn's handsome house in
town remained empty and deserted, and Aleck's country
agents received no orders to prepare his neglected estate
for a bride's arrival. Instead, returning from abroad, with
the utmost secrecy the two took up their abode in the
lonely house in the northern suburb where, from all hard-
won accounts, Severn returned to his "thinking" harder
than ever, and Marianne's prospects seemed those of living
burial. Outraged friends waited in vain for explanation or
invitation or advance of any kind; not only one "crank"
now but *two*, and people shook their heads and shrugged
their shoulders and deplored that Mrs. Severn had no near
kinsfolk to interfere.

Full of consternation and curiosity, Madame flew round
to the "hermitage," and insisted on an interview with a
determination that would accept no compromise nor
refusal.

When Marianne at length reluctantly appeared she
had not the bearing of a happy two months' bride, and
Madame told her so without any beating about the bush,
and in good round terms.

"What on earth did you marry him for?" she cried.
"Wasn't it to cure him, and instead of that you've let him
infect you, and here are the two of you now crazy together.
What does it mean?"

But when the good-hearted little matron fully understood what it did mean, her looks grew blank, and much she regretted having had anything to do with what must turn out an ill-omened match for at least one of the contracting parties.

"I thought at first that it would be easy to win him from himself," said the young wife, sorrowfully, "but I soon found that 'to think' is more to him than I am; I must either give him up, which is impossible, or share his seclusion, for no prayers or entreaties of mine can prevail on him to break it."

"But what in the name of wonder does he think about?"

"He cannot, or he will not tell me; but from the little I can gather, I imagine he ponders a great deal on the mystery of life. Once, in the early days of our marriage, he spoke to me of his parents, and said how strange it was that it should be in the power of two such beings to evolve so great a miracle as life. I think his brain is over-busy with the problem as to what life really is—the thing itself, I mean—actual existence."

Madame held up her hands aghast. "Someone ought to annul the marriage; the man is mad. Oh, Marianne, why did you do it? Come back with me this very day."

But the girl sadly shook her head.

"I would not undo it now if I could," she said; "I have failed in my hopes, but Aleck is not mad, and sane or mad, he is all the world to me. My fate is bound up in his, and I will live or die with him."

Madame shivered in her furs; there was something awful to her in this quiet acceptance of a fate. The room in which they sat was bright and neat and pretty, but a breath as from a charnal house seemed suddenly to blow across it, and a shadow of coming ill to darken the air.

"Ugh! I had rather you had died than have come to such a home as this," she said; "but for Heaven's sake, Marianne, if he will not listen to reason, do *you*, and leave this accursed place before harm happens to you." And so, shivering and moaning, she went away.

But a change was to come. Shortly after this Marianne Severn was awakened one midnight to find her husband standing by her bed; his eyes shone with an unholy radiance and his pale face glowed.

"I have found it," he cried, as she started up—"the idea, Marianne, that I have groped after for so long. Now, sweet, I have done with thinking, I must be doing! We will go back to the old life to-morrow, and I will make up to you all that you meant to sacrifice for your love's sake."

And in the happy tears that followed, Marianne realised the full weight of the burden, now, as she fondly hoped, lifted from her soul.

The return of Mr. and Mrs. Severn to the beaten tracks of society was a signal success. His lavish hospitality and *bonhomie,* her beauty and grace, and their joint wealth proved sure attractions in the enjoyment of which people forgot everything else, and if that fifteen months of "thinking" was ever referred to, no one laughed more heartily than Aleck himself. He did his best to make amends for lost time; his gentle melancholy and his studious habits were flung to the winds, and while always observing the bounds of decorum, pleasure seemed his sole pursuit. The many put this down to marriage and a natural reaction; the few said it would become debauchery, and prove the beginning of the hereditary end; but all were content to follow the lead, knowing that whichever way it went the luck was theirs—to be free agents in following.

And what of Marianne, the wife who would have thought the world well lost for her husband's sake?

She adored him still; he worshipped her, and no one thought her aught but happiest of the happy; yet, in truth, was she most miserable, moving always in the Valley of the Shadow of Dread. From her tender soul the burden had but been lifted to fall again with a more crushing weight. Aleck had given up thinking—true; but he had taken to doing; the lonely house in the northern suburb still owned him as master, and many a midnight, as she alone knew, he left her side to shut himself up in its solitude, to think no longer, but to *do*—what?

CHAPTER II.

AMONG the various items of news which filled the columns of the papers one bleak morning in March, was an insignificant paragraph setting forward in bold terms the discovery of the body of a murdered woman on the doorstep of a low lodging house in one of the worst localities of the East End.

At another time the tragedy might have been announced with big head-lines, and heralded by sensation, but the public mind was occupied with a foreign marriage and a Home Debate: it seemed likely that the French would blow up the South Coast with their new self-acting torpedo boat, and highly probable that an Anti-German riot was imminent among outraged out-o'-works: a murder was not wanted. The victim, moreover, proved to be an outcast whom no one even troubled to identify, and spite of the unusual and atrocious nature of the deed, the big dailies dismissed it with brief deprecation, while the lesser lights enlarged a little upon the state of things in general that allowed a murderer to escape with impunity from a neighbourhood perennially awake, and the body of his victim to grow cold, unobserved, on the threshold of a common lodging-house.

As to the wretched woman herself, no one gave a thought: her name even was never discovered, and in a week the whole thing was forgotten—save by two. One was Aleck Severn ....

Crouching, one Spring evening, on the lowest of the broad steps leading up to a lordly mansion in the West, was a wretched object that seemed to wither and shrink together as the cold, pale sun-finger touched it. From amidst a bundle of lamentable rags that revealed large patches of the blue and shivering flesh, a white, wild face was occasionally lifted to take a scared glance round, and at every approaching step a skinny arm curved itself quickly about the head as if to ward off an impending blow.

But nobody troubled about the wretch; foot-passengers were few, and the fashionable thoroughfare was crowded with carriages returning from the Park, whose occupants, descending one by one, at swiftly opening doors, took small heed of the Lazarus that sat at another Dives' gate. At length, as the sunshine died away and the east wind blew more bitterly, the outcast stirred himself, moaned feebly, and with a fearful glance over his shoulder, began dragging himself to his feet. At the same moment the door behind him opened, and a man, well-clad and wearing the easy assurance of wealth and standing, came slowly down the steps; he paused at sight of the wretch below him, and the tramp with his sudden fearful look directed upwards, paused too, crouching like some hunted dog almost at the other's feet.

" 'Twarn't me, boss," he muttered; "for God's sake, let me go! Gi' us a crust, boss; I'm nigh clemmed, dyin', and she's allus arter me; it's cruel."

Aleck Severn came down another step and peered closely into the youth's fever-bright eyes.

"So you know me?" he said.

"Yes, boss, I know ye, though it weren't the 'swell racket' ye were on to last time I seed ye. Gi' us something . . . I tell yer she were my sister . . . Lord, ye might help a cove."

And then Severn, quietly stretching out his arm, caught the wretch as he fell back in a death-like swoon.

Hastily summoned to his master's aid, Jenkins, most kind-hearted of his lofty class, lifted the bundle of rags and bones and bore it tenderly enough into the warm vestibule; he would have carried it, indeed, into his own little sanctum and taken all that was necessary on to his own shoulders, while his master went on his way, but that Mr. Severn negatived peremptorily.

"Don't make a fuss, Jenkins; just get a little brandy and say nothing about it. We can't keep the lad here; besides, he's been starved, and if we meddle we shall finish him. Bring an overcoat, too, to cover these rags. They'll take him in in a hospital I subscribe to, which will be quite the best thing for him. There, he is coming round—quick, get me a cab."

And so Jenkins brought brandy, overcoat, and cab, but was allowed to do no more. It was Mr. Severn himself who helped the waif down the steps, shut himself and his companion in, and gave the word of direction to the driver, which the butler did not hear.

"Master seems to be in a mighty hurry to get him off the premises," mused Jenkins. "Well, he wasn't much of a sight for females. Lucky for him he's fallen in Mr. Severn's way." And, with a sigh to his own balked philanthropy, the butler went below to tickle female ears with what the master had not thought fit for female eyes to behold.

CHAPTER III.

A FEEBLY burning taper illumined, with a ghostly light, an upper room in the house where Aleck Severn had once lived—thinking.

The chamber had been Marianne's during her short, sad tenancy of the place, and traces of her ownership remained in the feminine furniture, forgotten knick-knacks, and the dainty bed. On the latter was stretched a strange occupant.

Spite of the closely-cut hair, the pallid hands, and snow-white linen instead of dirty rags, Jenkins would have had no difficulty in recognising the waif who had fainted on his master's door-step; but Jenkins would have marvelled greatly at the nature of the hospital to which the master had taken him, and still more at the identity of the man, who, when the night was at its deepest, entered the room and crossed to the bed with the air of one who was at home there. It was Aleck.

Raising the taper and screening it with his hand, he looked down long and fixedly at the sleeper's face; it was that of a mere youth, scarcely more than a boy, and, under happier circumstances, might not have been without lines of beauty. Even now, worn and wasted with awful sickness, the mouth was tender, and the forehead showed intelligence and incipient capability.

"To think," muttered the watcher, "that *he* should have *put out* the very mystery that I am devoting my life one day to illumine."

Presently the sleeper stirred and opened his eyes; and, as their startled gaze met his, Severn saw in them recognition and reason.

"So you're better," he said quietly, putting down the light, "and you know me again?"

"Better, I don't know, I feel precious queer; but I know ye; oh, yes, Mister, I know ye."

"Ah, and can you remember when you last saw me?"

"Well, rather!" with a feeble laugh. "It wor last Saturday night as ivver wos, and you guv me 'arf a quid in the New Cut to tell you where Fanshawe's Jane hung out."

"Quite right; you have a good memory. What did you think I wanted with Fanshawe's Jane?"

"Lord save us, isn't she the pal of ivery bloke as can kiddy it; and don't she smash queer screens, and help on many a panic—I didn't think nothin' once I'd tuk your 'arf quid, guv'nor."

"No, you took me for something between a swell-mobsman and a burglar. But think again—that was the *first* time you saw me—try and remember the last."

There was a long silence; it seemed in the ghostly shadows as if Severn was gazing down upon the dead, then the youth's upturned look, startled at first, but clear, gradually grew wild and confused, and as the lapse of time was at length bridged over and memory recalled *all*, he started up with an awful cry, while the sweat of terror broke out in great beads upon his brow.

"Say, boss," he gasped in a husky whisper, "wher've ye brought me to? Do ye mean fair? I aint nivver 'armed ye, hev I? Say, ye've bin orful good; you'll let me go, won't ye, Guv'nor; for the love o' Gord, say ye will?"

"When you are strong enough. You have been very ill."

"Ill, hev I? Off my chump, I reckon; seems precious light. Say, Mister," and the husky voice became an almost inarticulate gasp, "did I *talk?*"

Severn's gaze held the wild eyes as if by a spell. "Yes, you talked a great deal," he said.

Shudder on shudder shook the youth's long frame; he

crouched back in the bed in an agony of terror, his jaw dropped, the words came with difficulty from between his rattling teeth.

"Boss, what did I say?"

Severn leant forward, and with a firm grasp pinioned the miserable creature's shaking hands.

"You said," and his tone scarcely seemed to break the silence, it was so low, and yet so impressive was it, that the words seemed to thunder back from the walls. "You said— enough to tell me who and what you are; your name is James Pate, and you are a *murderer*."

★   ★   ★   ★   ★   ★   ★   ★   ★   ★

"I cannot see why you should cling so to life," said Severn, a little later, when the first paroxysm of terror and agony was over, and the miserable Cain lay spent and breathing hard, "but I may as well tell you first as last that I am not one to save you from one death only to hand you over to another: if you value your life you shall have it—for me—partly because you are very young; partly because it is not *my* province to hunt you down, or give you up; and partly because I do not know that you are more unfit to live than many who will go scot-free to the end of the chapter."

"There is not even a search being made for you," Severn went on calmly, while the big tears of weakness and anguish rolled down the outcast's face and cheeks. "You shall stay here till you are well; then I will start you fresh, and help you to work out your own repentance. In your delirium you gave me an idea; it is the second idea I ever had in my life worth anything, and I am grateful: however, all you need understand now is that I mean to be your friend."

But it was long before the half-crazed brain could grasp more than the sense of its own mortal fear, and a wet and cheerless dawn was making yet more ghostly the surroundings of the strange interview, before Severn had made his meaning and his intentions plain.

Then, indeed, the creature grovelled, and would have licked the very dust off the feet of his preserver, but Aleck checked him with an imperturbable face.

"Do not be too grateful now," he said, "wait and see. I shall not keep you from the hangman's hands always for nothing. You are mine, body and soul, while you live, and perhaps you will live a very long time. Now I am going, and I shall not see you again till you are well enough to leave this place; but, understand me, if you try to escape me, I shall do something worse than hang you. Now sit up, and swear that you will never breathe your crime again in mortal ears, and that as soon as you can hold a pen you will write me a full confession of it; its every detail—the how and the why."

With a ghastly look on his youthful face the murderer swore, and as he sank back among the pillows, a bird outside the window burst into a sudden carol, clear and sweet; as if in answer, the rain-clouds broke, and the morning's first sunshine burst into the room.

"Who are you?" gasped Pate, turning his haggard eyes on Severn. "You tell me not to bless you. Are you man, or devil? Am I to *curse* you that you let me live?"

But Severn only smiled with gentle melancholy as he turned away.

"Time will show," he said.

CHAPTER IV.

The Confession of James Pate.

(*Note by Aleck Severn:* After reading this miserable and marvellous document, which I had to take down from his own lips, the man not being able to write, and having mused very considerably over it, I have induced two reflections.

Firstly, that in so far as man's conscience is his law and his motives his sins, I am perfectly justified in withholding this man from the imperfect dogmas of his kind.

Secondly, that the faculty for the wanton transmission and the wanton destruction of life inherent in the human race is totally at variance with the inestimable value we individually set upon it.) . . . . . .

. . . . "The Almighty knows it wasn't murder I had in my heart; don't larf, Guv'nor, I'll take my dyin' oath it's true. I ain't had such a feelin' as come over me then, afore or since, and sometimes when I think of my old home, and the bonnie red-cheeked lass as used to lead me by the hand o' Sundays, and set me on the bench inside the church door, with her arm around me to keep me from slipping, and my head a bumpin' agin her shoulder, I feel that I'd do it again, and she thank me for it, with her head bowed down like, an' her hands about my feet. But o' nights, Mister, that does it; she comes then; it doesn't matter where I dosses, nor what the crowd is, she comes then, always up *behind*, and she taps my shoulder; it's like a smart of flame, an' I turns an' sees her face. I knows as it was murder, *then*, Guv'nor, and I think of hell, and that *she'll allus be there, too.* She was

32

my sister, see? An' she loved me when I was a little kid.

"I'm nigh on to one-and-twenty, mister, for all that I don't look it. An' it's close on five years ago that I found things too slow down home, and I come up to London. I had a sister six year older nor me, and the prettiest wench for miles, and good enough to marry the parson. She—she didn't like my going; hung on to my neck at parting, and begged of me to think on her and 'Run straight, Jem,' says she, and she gave me a 'kerchief worked in with my name. 'Keep that,' she says, cryin', 'an' think o' Bessie, an' you won't go wrong.' Well, I tried agin' it, but from the first, Guv'nor, I was dead unlucky. Let me jest put a hand to anything, an' so sure's I did, it broke right up, till at last the coves fought shy of me; I couldn't find a job, nor I couldn't get a partner. I hawked an' cadged an'—starved. But I held on to that there 'kerchief of Bessie's through thick and thin, and felt soft like when I turned it, and sort of pray'd. My God! it's true, an' I had *it* an' no other, sure as I live, slung round my neck that night when the drunken blowen catched at it, and pulled down my face to hers an' kissed my cheek.

"It don't much matter lettin' on to you, Guv'nor, that 'twos Fanshawe's Jane first taught me how to thieve. I clemmed till I was nigh done for, an' then I was bold, and went at it desp'rate, an' luck turned. Lord! you never know'd such luck as mine; but the trade weren't in the blood, an' I never stomached it; thoughts of Bessie skeered me, and I think I should ha' tried to start fair and square agin but for one thing as happened. I came across a gel, Guv'nor; saw her a Sunday night outside a public—a lovely gel with a face as white as death, big eyes a burnin' in it, and fluffy hair all blowin' round it like shred gold. I went right down mad on her, then and there, an' it made no sort of odds to me that she was a thoro' paced bad 'un, and led me on deeper and deeper with one gang and another, 'till there was no cryin' off. So long as *she* was true, I didn't care, not I! I'd have eat the very dust she walked on. But there happened a time once I was laid up in 'orspital a spell, with a cut head as a bloke 'ad done for me in a fight a talkin' of her; she never come a-nigh me, Guv'nor, and when I dragged myself round again to her place, another cove was by her fire. She'd rounded on me. Down I went on my knees prayin' to her, or something like it; it nigh crazed me. 'Damn ye,' she says, 'do ye think I wanted you 'cept for what I could make out of ye for others? What should I want with a white-lipped sniffler like you?' And then she flung back her head and larfed; an', seeing her so, with her white cheeks an' her glowin' eyes lookin' so blasted pretty an' larfin'—at *me*—a something took me that was murder itself. I snarled like a dog, an'—'Knock him down, Bill,' says she, still larfin'—there, it sickens me; I'd sinned with her an' for her, I'd followed her beck like a dog, an' loved her true. It don't take much to knock a chap silly when he's as weak on his pins as I was. I went down like a skittle, she with her pretty head flung back, still a-larfin', larfin' an' larfin' . . . . When I come to my senses again the stars wos over me, an' the old cut in my head had opened, an' I was nigh blinded with blood. I sat up and cursed the jade, swallerin' my own blood to do it, an 'twas only the feel of Bessie's 'kerchief as kep' me back from makin' a hole in the river there and then . . . .

"After that I went on down'ards, steady like; I had no nouse in me to thieve even. I jest wandered round, thinkin' now and again that Bessie, as 'ad taken care on me when I was a kid, 'ud sure look me up afore I died; an' one night (it was the last day of Febr'y, an' Leap Year, for the girls joked on it) someone seein' me standin' shiv'ring outside a public—I got back there allus *once* atween night an' mornin'—it was there I'd first seen that damned wench with her white face an' shining eyes—took me in and gave me drink; the rest ain't clear; I was weak as a rat, an' the stuff fuddled me. Anyways, a woman comes up, a shawl pinned over her head; tips a wink to the others, claps her arm in mine, and leads me off. When *she* wor true—but, lord, now 'twos no manner of odds; I was pleased to ha' got company, and when the woman larfed, I larfed, and she larfed pretty often, and shouted, and cussed. She was dead drunk at last, and it was as much as I could do to roll wi' her into an old lumber yard, an' she dropped like a log on the timbers. An' at mornin', when it dawned, there came a sort of red glare all over the wood pile like fire; an' I starts up, dazed an' shiv'ring, then turns to see the wench. She slept still, her shawl a-fallen back, an' her face turned full to the red sky . . . . It was Bessie! . . . Oh . . . my . . . God!

"I dunno as I can rightly tell you any more, guv'nor. She was my sister; see? I thought of how she'd cared for me, an' how good she'd been, an' how I'd hung onto that 'kerchief, an' hoped to see her when I died. It was in my mind that she musn't wake an' know that it was me, her little lad, her brother! . . .

"The stake was handy, an' I struck an' struck agin. She never stirred. There was a little breeze a-blowin', an' her hair shook, an' her lips a-quivered as if she smiled. Oh, God Almighty! I carries her into the street, Guv'nor. I felt a sort o' glow, like shoutin' out an' fetchin' a crowd, but there was no one there. I heard a cock crowin' an' thought I was a kid agen, an' the red glare that as used to shine through the panes at Church, where she'd took me an' let me sleep, with my head on her arm . . . I lays her down on the first doorstep I come to, an' got away; I wasn't afeared, *then*, o' being caught, but, bye an' bye, when it was broad day, an' the people wos all shoutin' an' runnin', I got skeered. I asks a coffee-stall keeper what was up. 'A street walker done for,' says he . . . . Bessie!"

CHAPTER V.

WHEN Marianne and Aleck had been married the greater part of a year, the nameless trouble that lay at the heart of the gentle woman's life was intensified and a new grief added.

With no further explanation than she could gather from strangely expressed protestations and half-frenzied declarations of an unabated love, that yet could henceforth only show itself in renunciation, Marianne Severn was obliged to accept the fact that her husband was lost to her. True, she still shared his roof, his daily greeting was hers, and his daily attendance to one or more of their many engagements; but in all else he established himself as no more to her, save in the unswerving love she bore him, than any other of the many courteous men who frequented her home and paid homage to her wealth and beauty. His apartments were ordered separately and remote from hers, his incomings and outgoings unknown, his secret pursuits a mystery, and their brief married joy in each other left to become a dream. With unspeakable misgiving, Marianne saw in all this the growing outcome of the curse which, with the taint of madness and murder, the dying wretch who could call Severn her son had bequeathed to him. Once and again, on her knees, she besought him to tell her what it might mean.

The man answered her passionately, telling her in high-strung jargon that for his love he renounced her, and to save her from ill would go down childless to his grave. "A new race shall call me father," he cried, in a frenzy, "and hail me to all time."

"He is mad," thought Marianne, with inexpressible dismay; "he still loves me well enough not to kill me."

After such scenes had been once or twice repeated, she forbore further importunity, and set herself to bear the dreary days as best she might. She confided in no one, and the consolations other women might have found never occurred to her loving spirit, nor to a heart so filled with pity for her husband as to have no room for the sense of wrong towards herself.

As the summer deepened, and the heat grew unusually intense, Aleck used many endeavours to induce his wife to waive all other considerations and leave town at once, either for a country retreat or prolonged travel abroad. But on this point she was firm.

"It is bad enough for us to be apart as we are," she said, with gentle reproach; "but I could not bear the suspense and misery of actual separation. No, let me at least share the same house."

"You ought to curse the day you ever saw me," he answered. "The hand of Fate is on me; but why should I drag you into my doom? I love you still."

And, with a sickening heart, Marianne listened in silence, not daring to question more.

But about this time the longing seized upon her to revisit the garden where her pleading had once been fatefully successful. She knew that although much of the furniture had been removed, and the wholesome old housekeeper long since gone, the house was still in Aleck's hands, and day by day in her lonely distress the desire grew to pass through the familiar paths again, wander about the deserted rooms, and sit once more under the weeping ash, where she had come upon Severn that autumn day, like the sweet spirit of his dream.

There was also an unexpressed idea in her mind that perhaps in this particular spot some light might suddenly break in upon the mystery of her life, and some way be revealed to her by which she might save him, not now from the "*thought*," but from—oh woe—the *deed!*

After much hesitation, she expressed the wish to her husband, and in one of the formal interviews which constituted their daily intercourse, asked him for the key of the well-remembered garden door. To her dismay, the simple request was received with the first show of anger she had yet encountered. Severn not only roughly refused her the key, but in strong terms peremptorily forbade her to attempt any entrance to the house whatever, or even to go near it; adding, with uncalled for bitterness, that in her place, he should be only too glad to avoid the spot where, for her, so fatal a contract had been made.

Marianne's gentle spirit was roused: she turned on her husband with flashing eyes.

"If I went to that spot," she cried, "it would be indeed to mourn with bitter tears, that the love so freely offered and so freely taken, has availed nothing in saving one so bent on his own destruction and so unworthy of the prayers of a woman's true and devoted heart."

Then Severn, to whose mad soul she was still the one bright star that showed there was a Heaven, and whose very love for her compelled him to an act of self-renunciation the more heroic because never to be explained, tried with arguments and entreaty to remove the impression he had made.

"Scientific pursuits enthrall me," he said, "and it is as if fiends goaded me on to my goal: there is no drawing back, and I *will not draw back* for man or devil. But what need to shock your tender spirit by showing you my gloomy secrets. Would you have a vivisectionist for your husband, or know that these hands seek to solve the problem of life, with blood—and misery?"

And Marianne shuddered and shrank to the depths of

her being. At last, after self-communings that drove the sparkle from her eyes and hollowed out her youthful face, she resolved that she must watch her husband, and find out for herself what unholy project or fell work lay underneath these tragic hints, banishing her from his side by night and day. If she found herself deceived, and his grim words only a clever artifice to conceal wandering affection and the pursuit of dissipated pleasure, then her course was clear; but if her hideous presentiments were confirmed, and she discovered her husband to be all she dimly feared, then would she trust to Heaven and her own devotion to show her the way to deal.

CHAPTER VI.

LYING in wait for such an opportunity, one evening Marianne overheard an order which her husband was giving to his servant, the valet, a well-trained man, who was discreet, and used to his master's freaks and vagaries. The orders given informed her that Severn was intending to be absent all night, and to return between seven and eight the next morning. Marianne laid her plans.

"I cannot sleep," she said to her maid, "and I have been told to try what a walk will do taken in the very early morning. Put me out something suitable now, and to-morrow do not come till I ring, then bring me some hot coffee. I shall let myself in by the side door; Madame will accompany me by arrangement, so there will be no need of your escort. Good-night, Christine, and sleep well."

And Christine went away content, and thought her mistress's plan so natural that she did not even concern herself to repeat its nature in the servants' quarters.

Marianne's glib lies gave her sensitive feelings some compunction; but, as regards Madame, she consoled herself by reflecting that this cheery friend, who knew more of the skeleton in her cupboard than anyone, would joyfully lend her name to any or every scheme that had her friend's peace of mind in view.

Sitting alone in sad meditation, with her window open to the night, Marianne heard her husband leave the house, and, leaning forward, bating her very breath in her excitement, she saw the familiar figure, distinct, though etherealized in the soft moonlight, cross the road. There a second figure came out of the shadows of a portico to meet it—a slight, youthful figure, with a nervous, restless air, and a look that, even at that distance and in the deceptive light, seemed to the watcher's eager eyes to wear the unquestioning adoration and dumb devotion of a dog.

As the two passed rapidly away and out of sight, the unhappy woman sank down with a sob.

There was no need for her to start in pursuit of the men, even had it been feasible. She was certain in her own mind whither they were bound; it only remained to know on what errand.

Between the fever of excitement and the chill of dread, the slow hours passed till the red and gold of the unseen dawn was reflected in the sky; then, with trembling fingers, Marianne arranged herself in the sober garments ready for her, and when the first sunbeam touched the eastern window she shrouded her face in a thick veil, and with all the timidity of an unaccustomed thief stole through the unfamiliar grey silence and desertion of the house, down stairway, through hall, vestibule, and out into the open street. There her spirits somewhat revived, the air was so golden bright, the aspect of all about her so serene. Hurling into less fashionable thoroughfares, where busy people were already up and astir, Marianne had not travelled far before a passing cab was at her service. A liberal fare, and hurry, urged on account of illness, together with a horse fresh from the stables, worked wonders, and it lacked still some twenty minutes of six when Marianne came to a standstill before the garden door of the lonely house in the deserted road. She had dismissed her driver at a little distance, and not the slightest evidence of life met her, save that the fresh sunshine danced on the leaves of the acacias and the limes above the wall, and that there was company in the lark's joyous carol overhead. As she stood thus hesitating, her hand upon the yielding latch of the door, suddenly a long, low wail broke through the stillness and echoed with awful meaning in the stricken listener's ears.

There was another, and yet another, and then—a silence that spoke.

For a full minute the woman leaned against the wall, sick unto death, so she thought; then a wholesome rush of burning indignation revivified her, and she pushed the door open and boldly entered the garden. Within, all was changed from the vision of her remembrance. Everything bore the direful aspect of things once cared for given over to neglect and decay: the grass grew lank and luxuriant, and the trim path was scarcely discernible, while the unchecked shrubs had grown apace, and gave the place a dark and sombre air, the roses adding a mournful plaint as unnoticed they blossomed and died. But scarcely had Marianne had time to note all this, and take a few already hesitating steps forward, when the sound of approaching voices put her bold resolves to flight, and, in unreasoning terror, allowing herself no instant for reflection, she swiftly stepped behind some thick arbutus bushes standing near.

People in hiding, be their purpose high or low, their motive good or ill, are each and all the victim of a species of terror peculiarly their position's own. The unhappy Marianne felt the truth of this in full as she crouched there with bated breath, every rustle of the leaves about her making her heart leap as though it must burst itself within her throat.

There was a tacit pause as the speakers reached the garden door. Marianne had left it unfastened; the fact seemed to escape them. They were conversing earnestly, but at first in tones so low and guarded, that not even her straining ears, but a few yards away, could catch more than the tone of the one, so dear and so familiar, and of the other, rough and uncultured, heard for the first time. As the minutes passed, however, the listener gained enough courage to slightly part the boughs and peer cautiously through at the two men, though she had not needed the proof of her eyes to tell her who they were. Her husband stood the nearer to her, sideways, supporting himself against an acacia tree. His face was upturned to the bright sky, and wore a sad, unfathomable look; on the temple and the cheek were two small and irregular crimson smears. Opposite her was the youth she had seen in the moonlight, the dumb devotion and adoration, palpable even then, very visible now. The face was pale and haggard, bearing the signs of a wasting disease, and this, together with the expression with which the blue eyes were riveted on Severn, redeemed to some extent the air of vulgar breed which the comfortable, almost stylish, attire could not obliterate. It was evident that the vigils of the night had told on both: the conversation flagged, and there was a long pause, as if from utter weariness. At last the young man broke silence again, baring his head to the breeze with a weary sigh.

"Say, boss," and from his lips the words sounded like a reverential endearment, "you've done your last at this sort of thing?"

"Yes, it can help me no longer." Severn's gaze was still fixed on the bright sky.

"And, boss, what is it to be next?" The tone was indescribable. It brought Aleck's eyes down quickly to his companion's face; he laid his hand gently on the young man's shoulder.

"Are you ready for it, Jem?" he asked.

The response was there in Jem's adoring eyes, but he answered as well.

"I'm ready, an' ye know it; but oh, if ye'd only stop; not fer me; it can't matter fer me, but fer yer own sake; I sha'n't live long, an' who'll help ye then, an' yer fancies 'ull drive ye mad, an' git ye inter trouble."

Jem threw into the homely words a pathetic and awful earnestness that gave them terrible weight.

"Say no more," said Severn; "the die is cast, and our Fates are intertwined; but at the day of reckoning I will absolve *you*, Jem; on my head will be the guilt, and on my lips will be the answer. But there never will be a day of reckoning, my lad; I am begotten of a fiend; a fiend bore me, and cursed me; the fiend-life that is in me is fore-doomed! what matter, then, to what purpose I put it! There is a moment when life begins, whatever life may be, and that moment I mean one day to seize, and once for all to understand!" . . . . . .

"There is some of the blood on your face," said Jem; "let me wipe it off for you, boss."

His own was ghastly-pale; his thin fingers trembled; he was blood-stained, too, in a deeper sense, but Aleck Severn, gazing with his own intellectual and haunted soul, through those faithful eyes, into the heroism and devotion of the spirit that lay beneath, shuddered as a born denizen of hell may shudder *once* when he hears the portals of hope close *for ever* behind some trusting soul he has enticed to wander there for a brief spell.

"I almost wish you were dead, Jem," he said, and then they passed out of the garden together.

Strangely enough, Marianne Severn's first clear thought, when her shocked senses had gathered themselves together, was that of jealousy. She was jealous of that pale youth who was "ready," and on whom her husband had looked with such strange affection.

"Was *I* not a tool ready to his hands," she murmured, holding her racked head, as she walked dizzily up the path towards the house; "rather than that another's devotion should win his heart, and that another should be the recipient of his secrets, so that he shuts me out, I would have waded with him through seas of blood. He cares for me no more, and I would die for him."

At first her thoughts went no further than the horror

of the vivisectionist, and the purpose of her husband's warped life seemed plain enough; but when the first pangs of baffled love had subsided, she reflected that what might shock her so much would not others, and that the mere fact of Aleck Severn being a disciple of vivisection, for what private ends and aims soever, was not enough to account for isolated months of gloomy reverie, his painful separation from herself, his wild and fanatical words, nor the mysterious tie which bound him to so strange and unlikely a companion. No, some deeper horror lay behind. She could not doubt it. Some hideous endeavour to which the pursuits licensed by Science were but a means to a still unattained end . . . . The house stood silent and deserted amid its unpruned creepers. "What a charming retreat might be made here," would have been the cry of a casual observer, but Marianne took no heed of the roses and the honeysuckle that brushed her with their dewy lips and stretched out arms as if to detain and comfort. With trembling haste she tried the doors, but all were closely fastened and barred. Not a sound came from within; an upper window was open, and a white curtain waved there like a beckoning hand. But to enter that way was impossible. Passing round the house, she found every means of admission not only closed but shuttered, with the exception of the window belonging to her husband's former study. This opened, door-like, on to the verandah which skirted the front of the house, and, door-fashion, was locked from the outside, this probably being the way chosen for ingress and egress. But, though unshuttered, the grey blind was down, and effectually concealed any glimpses even of the room within.

The bright sunshine all about, the flowers, the song of the birds, the familiar aspects, gave Marianne a faint sense of company and a momentary boldness. Raising the light stick she had armed herself with before leaving home, she brought it down with force upon one of the upper panels: the glass shivered and cracked from one end to the other, but only a comparatively small portion broke completely away, and fell with a clatter on to the pavement of the verandah. To the woman's strained ears the noise seemed appalling, and for a moment she crouched in breathless expectancy, prepared to flee; but the peace of the deserted garden continued unbroken; not a sound came from within or without the silent house, and presently, with the precaution of a thief, she inserted her hand into the jagged aperture. There was barely room for the wrist to turn without danger, but with much patient manipulation she managed at length to grasp the blind in her fingers and draw it aside.

The room was bare of any carpet or furniture, save two deal chairs, and a table of complicated make that filled up the centre. On this, *in a sitting posture*, was a shrouded something that faced towards the window: the cloth that wrapped it bore a few such crimson stains as those that had flecked Severn's brow and chin . . . .The cloth stirred; it was being lifted by the breeze! The awful upright figure moved—it rose—it came towards her—it was close! . . . Let the blind drop—it was there behind it! Quick, a freed wrist, ere it is laid hold on from within. God, help me to get away!! . . . . A few staggering steps along the verandah, and then Marianne fell, faint and dizzy, to her knees. Oh, Heaven, have mercy!

* * * * * * * * *

It was well after nine when Mrs. Severn rang for her maid and the hot coffee she had ordered overnight: the servants had seen her some little time before part from Madame at the side entrance, and walk quickly upstairs to her room. Christine found her lying, dressed, on the bed, and looking pale and wan; she ventured to say that she thought so unusual a walk had not done her mistress much good.

"No," was the answer, "I do not think I shall try it again; never mind my dress, I cannot move; bring your work and sit where I can see you, till I fall asleep."

This was an unusual order, and Christine wondered, but after a time got used to even closer attendance, and, in course of time, confided to the genial butler that she believed her mistress was "afraid"—of what, or why, she could not say.

It was pitiably true; Marianne's nerves had been shaken beyond repair: after a time, reason somewhat reasserted itself, and in her long self-communings she told herself that what she had seen, if ghastly enough, could no doubt be naturally and simply explained. But still she could not bear to be alone; the dark was peopled with forms of unspeakable dread: wails of pain echoed in her ears, and her husband's melancholy, handsome face haunted her pillow like the embodiment of coming doom.

CHAPTER VII.

IT was a January day, between nine and ten o'clock at night, early in the month, and bitter weather. The excitement of the White Festival was over; a depressed air marked the few shops that were still open, and the street passengers hurried by only intent to get to their homes. There were very few pedestrians of any sort abroad, and the couple who, as the clock struck ten, emerged from a cheap restaurant in a quiet part of Islington found they had the pavement to themselves. They were man and woman, the man dark, with a three days' growth of black stubble on chin and cheek, and clad in comfortable ill-cut clothing. The woman was young, and, to some eyes, pretty, but depravity and coarseness were there in every line of her face and every turn of her head, while her dress and style bore an unmistakable stamp. But the profusion of yellow, fluffy hair, the deep, dark eyes, and the white, even teeth, were natural beauties that while youth remained no degradation could obliterate. The two stood shivering in the bitter blast a moment, then the girl impatiently tugged at her companion's arm. Her face was flushed: she seemed to have been plied with drink.

"What's the racket?" she cried, noisily, "what's this move fur? Ain't ye goin' ter git a cab? Wot's the use of it all if yer not? Ho, hi, cabby there! don't yer want ter give a real lady a ride—wait fer the duchess, can't ye?"

But before she had time to know her own purpose, or do more than barely raise her voice, the man's hands had closed on her arm with a grip of steel; they were not particularly white—nor even particularly clean—hands, but they were wonderfully well-shaped and slim, and the words that enforced the grip, though rough and coarsely uttered, were not in the tone of even a superior mechanic.

"Look here, Polly," he said, dragging her into the shadows, "the stuff you've been having has got into your head; but don't let it master you for your own sake. I'm going to take you home with me to-night; but we're not going to take a cab—that is all to come. We shall walk every inch of the way, and the first time you raise your voice I'll hand you over to the police. Now, take my arm."

The girl was cowed in a moment, and sobered; but the look in her face as she raised her head was only slightly that of fear.

"I wonder why you ever took up with me," she said, humbly. "I'm all right, guv'nor, never you fear; and as for cabs, I'd rather hev your arm than all the cabs that ever wos."

The man seemed to scowl.

"Well, here it is," he said, ungraciously, "and now step out—we have a goodish bit to go."

As eleven o'clock struck, the key turned in the garden door of a certain suburban dwelling, and Polly and her companion entered side by side. The girl had been better than her word; she had walked all the way in perfect silence, and with unflagging step; now her grasp tightened, and as their footsteps crunched along the frosty path, she whispered, "Is this your home?" in a gasp of awe-struck dismay.

There was no greenery now, or flowers, to add romance, with rustle of leaves and scent of blossoms; the house stood gaunt and bare, in the starlight, and the skeleton trees rattled their branches in the blast. The girl shivered.

"Ugh! it do look glum," she said, trying a reckless laugh.

"Wait till you get inside," was the answer; "at any rate, there you will find warmth and light." Still drawing her with him, the man passed round the house and tapped softly at the great dark glass door that had once been broken by Marianne Severn's hand. In instant response the shutters were withdrawn, and the window opened; a flood of light rushed out, and ere Polly's dazzled eyes could recover from the shock, or she herself be distinctly seen, the slam of a door close at hand, announced that the third person had only awaited the summons to answer it, and then disappear.

Polly thought she was about to connive at a burglary, or enter a swell-mobsman's retreat. She was not in the least afraid. Always under the same disguise, Severn had been known to her for many months, and rough wooer, rough master, as he had always been, she owed to him all that had ever even approached the gracious or good in her life, and, vicious as she was, she was not without sense of gratitude. She trusted the man implicitly, and under his unconscious influence had made some rough attempts to renovate her ways.

"Now you can make yourself comfortable," said Severn, as he barred and bolted the shutters behind them.

Midnight struck, reverberating from half-a-dozen different steeples. The girl lay asleep in front of the glowing, leaping fire. Repose softened the harshness of her face, her cheeks were flushed, her lips parted, her bosom rose and fell peacefully; in the rich light her gaudy dress looked only bright, not garish, and the arm that was flung above her tumbled hair was white and smooth. In its way the whole was a picture of unconscious and trustful prettiness that must have pleased even the censorious; but Severn's gentle, gloomy eyes were turned on her with a thoughtful gaze in which admiration had no part.

For some reason he had removed his disguise, and was in evening dress; his face was pale and melancholy, but composed. He ran one hand through his soft brown hair as he mused over his victim.

There were no candles in the room, but they were

not needed: the light from the huge fire glowed in every corner: the atmosphere had become like that of a forcing house. In time the sleeper seemed to feel the oppression, and stirred uneasily; her breath came with difficulty. But the man sat on undisturbed, though his own cheeks grew flushed and the moisture started to his brow. When the minute hand of the noiseless clock above him was pointing to a quarter past the hour, he rose, and moved softly about the room. On the table were a decanter and glasses: the girl had had more wine before falling asleep—wine that had been drugged, for, taking up a tiny goblet of a deep Bohemian red in which some liquid still remained, Severn dropped it whole into the white hot heart of the huge fire.

Whatever of horror Marianne Severn might have thought to discover in this room months before, there was nothing now in its general character to denote that it served otherwise than as an ordinary sitting-room or study: the strange looking table was gone, the corners were empty, the sleeping, dishevelled woman and the glowing fire would seem to point only to sensuous repose.

Severn moved silently to and fro, horribly composed. Once, approaching the girl, he laid his hand lightly on the yellow hair. "Is it worth while?" his brain was asking, and he paused to think. "After all, there was no end to the puzzle: life is movement: when a thing voluntarily moves it lives: the first movement is life. But is it? What is *movement*? A toad lives motionless a thousand years, an infant is stillborn: where is the *vital* difference in the process of *their* production? Life is of no value as a gift: its creation is a common impulse shared with the meanest of crawling things, but it is priceless as a possession." With this reflection came a momentary pang of compunction. "After all," he muttered again, "is it worth while? Suppose I do succeed, will success ever still the racking torture of the devil that berides me?"

Severn fell into a deeper, and yet deeper thought. The touch of compassion vanished from lip and brow, and the devilish idea that was in his mind seemed dearer and clearer than ever.

The girl moved and moaned, throwing up her arms wildly above her head. Severn stooped suddenly and kissed her.

"After all, you will have the least to do with it," he said, with a curious smile.

Heaping on more coals till the flames rushed up with a roar, and the big drops rolled down the troubled sleeper's face, Severn consulted a thermometer that hung on the wall. The result was satisfactory, and, with more despatch than he had hitherto displayed, he proceeded to complete his preparations. They were few, but significant, and showed an awful forethought.

"Wake, sleeper—wake and pray. Look you, here is murder!" . . . .

* * * * * * * *

It was a face changed almost beyond recognition that thrust itself into the room in answer to Severn's cautious call; livid and drawn, corpse-like, with blue lips that had no strength to shut in the chattering teeth, and starting eyes that were mute witnesses to the horror within; but there was no hesitation, nor holding back, no appeal nor reproach. Severn lightly flung a handkerchief over the woman's face. With a steady step the young man came forward to the centre of the room. There he paused, and kept his dilated eyes fixed full and solely upon his master.

"You're ready, boss?" he said, thickly, and with difficulty; "then say the word, I'm here."

Severn was fingering a knife. There were two more on the table—one very long and curved and edged like a razor. They glittered evilly, blue and red. The man looked at the youth half contemptuously, half in admiration.

"I can't do without you, Pate, or I would. I'm afraid, by your looks, my reasonings haven't done you much good."

"My hands are steady, boss; I won't fail you; but I can't feel about it as you do. I s'pose you're right—I won't fail you!"

"You think I'm the devil, or something worse," said Severn, with a shadowy smile.

"I dunno," was the answer, given with a simplicity that rendered it not absurd. "Sometimes, when I think on it all, I hopes you are."

"Why, Jem?"

"'Cos then I'll be bound to see you some times, even when I get to hell!"

Severn did not meet this with even the shadow of a smile: for a moment he felt the shock of its meaning, but things went too deep with him. He could not be swayed by mere impressions.

"Truth to thy soul, thy soul shall save," he quoted, then, laying his hands on the other's shoulder, and looking with much tenderness into his eyes, he added—

"It was an original thought made hell: only *original* sinners can people it. Now, Jem!"

Jem did not understand the words, but he did the look: the sense of the impossibility of it came over him anew—this gentle, melancholy, learned man, with so tender a touch and soft a tone—this man a nameless fiend!

"Oh, boss, if it were only to die myself!" The words leaped from his agonised white lips; but, as knowing they were futile, he waited for no response, but straightened himself up, prepared.

The girl now lay perfectly still, her hands hanging down inert at her sides. The handkerchief still concealed the face: there was no sound whatever to indicate life. With a mighty effort, Jem turned towards the chair, took a step forward and raised his eyes. He started visibly, the drawn face grew more pinched and livid; he pointed to the yellow, fluffy hair.

"Look," he stammered, "*her* hair wur like that," and he made a movement as if he would have bared the face. Severn interposed.

"No need, no need," he said, "no good to see her face again. Jem," he added, more quickly, stooping close to the recumbent figure, "quick, pile on more fuel, and help me to move her. Quick, not a moment must be lost—she is dead already."

★　★　★　★　★　★　★　★

A clock sounded the dismal hour of two.

The horror was accomplished, and Aleck Severn's fiendish hope remained as far removed as ever!

One! two! The telling sound seemed to re-echo in the very room itself; there was a rush as of footsteps in the room overhead, a ghostly sound as of voices moaning at the keyhole, a wrathful shrieking in the air without.

Jem Pate's face had grown old, very old; his form was shrunk and bowed, a greyness had fallen upon his cheeks and hair.

"Now you've done with her, boss, I'll take a look at the face," he said, in a strange tone.

Severn was standing motionless and apart, wrapped in a gloomy reverie. At Jem's voice he lifted his eyes—those sane and gentle eyes—in a slightly startled way. There had been no speech for more than an hour, and the silence in the room had only been broken by the crackling of the fire and a ghastly sound as of dripping rain.

"I can look now?" said Jem again, as their eyes met.

"Yes, and then let's get her away. I see you know who it

is. Well, she laughed at you once, Jem, and the laugh nearly sent you to the gallows; she laughed at me this time, and the laugh has cost her her life."

She looked—*dead*. It was a shock to withdraw the 'kerchief and find the eyes wide open and staring beneath. There was no coarseness in the face now, nor scarcely beauty, nor even repose—only death that with icy fingers had written "murder" from brow to chin.

"Right enough, it's her," whispered Jem; then he looked at the whole of the sight before him, and fell to shivering and shaking, and stumbled forward, as if gone blind, with a thick and stifling sound . . . .

At last Severn roused himself. In all his sullen disappointment he remembered the practical part of the night's work was yet to come. Little by little, exercising all his curious power, he soothed the youth into an apathetic calm, and before another hour had chimed the body was gone, the fire out, the house deserted and empty; while in the bitter blast of the howling night two men fought their way back from a lonely field where they had left a hideous something staring up into the dark with glassy eyes into which the icy rain drops pattered.

And from that hour on Jem Pate was dumb.

CHAPTER VIII.

"THE consideration of murder in the abstract opens up a wide field for reflection," said Severn, delicately discussing a very elegant lunch, within a few yards of the club fire. "For instance, you are a Positivist. You hold that this life is all; then your creed should hold murder in special abhorrence, and the man who drowns a dog as guilty as he who mangles a maid. On the other hand, I am a fatalist. I find nothing to be said about it at all; the victim only accomplishes a pre-destined fate that is inevitable, and the murderer is the unhappy instrument, wil-he, nil-he. So on, in infinite variety."

The man addressed laughed softly. Severn had a melancholy, beneficent way even about his disquisitions, and it was slightly amusing to hear him discussing murder with so much aplomb, for it was well-known among his intimates that he hated the sight and smell of blood, and never handled a gun.

"Very good, my friend," said the man addressed, "and you are so far right that there are murders and murders; but this particular case in point is something more than mere destruction of life—the girl was most foully butchered by a fiend."

"Ha, I thought Jenkins was gloating with great unction over the paper this morning, but I have not looked at it myself. What are the details?"

"Nay, read them for yourself, my boy," and the man addressed rose, stretched himself, and sauntered off, before long to be drawn into the same gossip elsewhere, for the whole town rang with the horrible tale, and theories anent it were the fashion of the hour.

Taking up the paper, Aleck Severn turned to the account, and read it from beginning to end attentively. Shorn of all verbiage, it amounted indeed only to a few bare facts. Late on the preceding afternoon (Saturday) a lad of about sixteen, wandering aimlessly (so he affirmed) in some deserted building-lots to the north of London, and amusing himself by throwing stones at stray cats and chasing them, was attracted by a hideous-looking object which lay extended on the grass near a ditch and a broken hedge. Fearing to approach, the boy fled, and summoned the assistance of a cowman, who was stalling his cows in some sheds not very distant. The man, hurrying to the spot, found the body of a young woman, fully dressed, with the exception of bonnet or shawl. The body presented an awful appearance, the face having been completely gnawed away by dogs or rats, presumably the latter. The hair was abundant, and of a natural pale yellow, but was saturated with water, as were the clothes, there having been recent and heavy rains; the hands were fairly well-cared for, and showed no signs of manual labour. A large crowd soon gathered, and the police were quickly on the spot. After the body had been removed to the nearest mortuary, an examination discovered the fact not only of a most frightful murder, but of indescribable mutilation. The lower part of the body had been left carefully enwrapped in coarse linen, which was much stained. "The novelty of the crime, and its (presumably) highly unusual motive attract great attention. The total obliteration of the face will render identification difficult; the police at present have no clue, etc." So much, and thus, the papers, with much more anent the mysterious absence of any cry heard by those living near, in spite of the terrific fact that there were no other wounds in a vital part, and no proof that the wretch had been even smothered before being mangled, as well as the locality chosen, and the utter absence of any trace of how the murderer or murderers had brought their victim thither. That the murder had not been done on the spot seemed conclusive on many grounds, the utter absence of blood foremost.

Severn read the whole through several times with a gradually sobering face, then he folded up the paper, rose, pushed back his chair, and walked to the door with the deliberate but steady air of one who has come to a grave resolution. In the vestibule, as he stood drawing on his gloves, he was joined by a young man who particularly affected his society; they walked together down the steps and into the street.

"Which way, Severn? Can you manage with my company?"

"If you care to participate in a gloomy errand. I am on my way to the D Police Station."

"Great Powers, what for? That's where they've got that poor girl."

"I know it; and, do you know, I think I must have been one of the last persons to see the unhappy creature alive. I am going there to give information; it may lead to a clue. You see, I have been in the habit lately of spending a good deal of time at a small place I have in the near neighbourhood of the spot where the body was discovered."

"Well?"

"Well, it amounts to very little, but it may be worth mentioning. I was hurrying along a lonely road that leads to my quarters there at about a quarter to eleven on Friday night, when I was rather surprised to notice a couple, evidently on amorous terms, strolling towards me. It surprised me, I say, for it was neither the night nor the place for sweethearts. The man had his arm about the woman's shoulders. They staggered a good bit as they walked, and, concluding they were both tipsy, I went into the middle of the road to give them a wide berth; without meaning to do so, I noticed at the same moment, as they lurched near a lamp, that the woman was young, with a quantity of yellow hair all tumbled about her face. The man was a broad, burly fellow, but I did not observe him so closely—naturally, perhaps. He was dark, with a stubbly beard, and rather long hair falling on his neck. I think he wore earrings, and had a generally broken-down air about him. I have little doubt he was the murderer, and the girl with him the victim."

"But the mutilation, the wrapping of the body, the other horrors?" gasped his companion.

Severn shrugged his shoulders. "True; it is altogether a baffling mystery; still, in the interest of justice, I had better mention the little I know."

The wealthy Mr. Severn's story was listened to with deference, and the clue accepted with eagerness. Not waiting to be questioned, Aleck, further, fully explained his own presence in the neighbourhood, and the scientific pursuits which long habits of seclusion and private study had led him to carry on in retirement at his former residence. He was congratulated on the clear method he had followed in telling what he had to tell, and won further praise by offering a private reward of a handsome sum to anyone bringing to light the perpetrator of the atrocity.

Through a malformation of one foot, the hideous corpse lying in the parish mortuary was finally identified as having once been the animate form of one calling herself Polly Dean, who for some years past had made herself notorious in certain quarters of the East End as a kept woman of professional burglars, swindlers, and blacklegs generally. At the inquest there were many to uphold Severn's testimony, and to depose as to Polly's intimacy with the stubbly-chinned, foreign-looking, burly, long-haired individual he described.

Severn himself was one of the witnesses called. As the

horrors of the surgical examination were unfolded Aleck turned white and faint.

"Good God," he muttered to the acquaintance next him, "what would you feel like if you'd loved that woman?"

"Don't," returned the other, uneasily. "Fortunately, no one loved *her*."

"I once heard of a man stricken dumb at the fate of a woman he cared for," whispered Aleck, wiping his brow.

"Ah, she must have been of a different sort to that doomed wretch," was the reply; for the speaker was conventional. Most people are . . . .

Mr. Severn's voluntary statement in connection with the murder invested him with a sort of second-rate personal interest in it, and, speculation running high as to the motive for the appalling deed, his particular theory was asked for by every acquaintance he met, and eagerly discussed afterwards, as if it were weighted with special authority.

"I do not consider it the outcome of mere brutality," said Severn, with a curious gleam in his melancholy eyes, "and I don't think a lethargic Saxon had much to do with it. You may put it down to be the work of some broken-down foreign student who wants to put into force some cherished idea—some craze about the embryo of things; it is murder by a madman, but one who has nothing less than life in view."

This being something near the truth, was consequently dismissed as untenable, and a dozen other theories were hazarded, but the only fact that could be arrived at with any certainty was that of the *utter incompetency of the general mind to grapple with any subject that leads even one step aside from the beaten track.*

The woman was buried and forgotten. Men are very finite in the interest they take in things, and if a fellow creature were to rise from his grave to-morrow he would be speedily forgotten, and have to resort to the variety stage if he wanted to make resurrection pay.

Among others, Severn himself grew impatient at last of even a casual mention of the horror, and declared that the cunning murderer must be laughing in his sleeve at the vast talk-draped skeleton of incompetency, which was all his crime had evoked.

CHAPTER IX.

AND now, strangely enough, in the spring that followed, when all the world was bright, and young life answered to young life with throbbing veins and joyous heart, Marianne's love rose again supremely towards her husband, and she wooed and won him a second time.

The news of the murder, and the fact of its locality, had at the moment given her an uneasy shock, but Aleck's subsequent action in the matter, the humane and honourable light in which she saw him represented and heard him spoken of, swept the seeds of suspicion from her "one-folded" and infatuated mind, and as the days rolled on, and the effects of that fateful night when she had dogged him more and more declined, she, too, forgot that yellow-haired and mutilated woman, and felt, with the youth about her, her own youth and her love renewed.

"This barrier between us is perfectly absurd," she said to her tried friend, Madame. "Are we both to live for ever apart when we love each other? I was content when I had deluded myself into believing there might be some cause for it into which I had better not enquire; but now I am sure it is all a misunderstanding. Aleck is morbidly inclined, and over-sensitive, and my behaviour has foolishly encouraged him. Whatever he may do, it has the sanction and approval of science, and I shall be a fool to let science be a successful rival any longer. Besides, my lonely life is insupportable: I begin to see ghosts, and commit murder in my sleep."

Carried away by her new enthusiasm, Marianne forgot many things which ought to have retained their significance, and Madame, though she had heard of most of them, had not the heart to damp her new beauty and her ardour. She bade her follow the dictates of her mood. And so the yellow moon of the daffodil month, the dust of whose days is precious, smiled down upon the young wife's second honeymoon.

Aleck was not difficult to win; like many warped and introspective brains he could act strongly in supposititious cases. He could resist temptation as he presented it to himself; he could scarcely refrain when it came to him powerfully in "objective" fashion.

Though the paradoxically successful failure of his first experiment had fearfully developed his bent, he still secretly adored his wife, and in the period of inactivity and re-action that followed the murder he was just in the mood to very willingly yield to the renewed tender of her love.

Had she remained aloof, the most sacred part of his feelings for her would have kept him a stranger to her till the end; but now he silenced his own arguments with his own crime, and when she gathered him in her arms, and vowed that nothing so commonplace as science should estrange them any more, he answered with a closer clasp, and long unused words of love.

"Only you might have trusted me, Aleck," she murmured. "You tell me you are the son of a murderess: I tell you that were you yourself a murderer, I would rather share your doom than a happy lot with any other man!"

She was very beautiful, very infatuated, and carried away by her own words.

Aleck half-believed, and for a moment hesitated, while confession almost rushed to his lips. Then he laughed in self-derision as he kissed her—"Jem Pate was truer than any woman, and—was dumb!"

The months that followed this re-union brought a time of perfect bliss to Marianne, for even the faint foreshadowing of evil which had troubled her in her first wedded days was gone.

Her heaven was serene, her husband doubly hers again, neither "thinking" nor "doing," and with the noontide of the summer came the noontide of her content, for the once abandoned hope of Motherhood came to nestle at her heart, and her measure of happiness was pressed down and running over.

"And so you are beatified at last?" said Madame, and Marianne answered with a look.

"I should never have doubted," she said.

"But she will have to doubt again, and then it will kill her," reflected Madame, who possessed at certain times the peculiarity found in corns: in the most brilliant weather she could forebode rain . . . .

With September, Aleck and his wife returned from foreign travel to their home in town, and one afternoon shortly after, Marianne, being alone with her husband, and he in lover-like mood, she was impelled, so that the last cloud might be dissipated between them for ever, to make full confession of her visit to his suburban retreat, her discovery there, and its subsequent effect.

Being now secure in her happiness, she treated the whole affair lightly, expressing her contrition and asking for pardon with pretty grace. She ended by a reference to the youth she had seen with her husband in the garden, and had been jealous of. She had almost forgotten him, she said: now she wanted to know where he was.

Aleck, in his turn, seemed exceedingly amused with his wife's tale. He laughed loudly, as if the idea of her playing the spy upon him tickled him immensely; he rubbed his hands in glee as she touched, in playful rebuke, on what she had seen, softened now to memory by lapse of time; and when she spoke of the youth, he declared, with a guffaw, that she should see him for herself that very day, and blow with her own sweet breath the last odour of mystery out of the lonely house in the northern suburb.

The fact that a chance word from his wife might have imperilled his position, and that her knowledge of Pate's existence and devotion might cause dangerous contingencies to arise in the future added devilish zest to the contemplation of the second crime, which Severn was even then turning over in his brain. He found delight in disarming suspicion by anticipating it, and in baffling inquiry by courting it. He held that candour is the best disguise for guilt, and that a well-planned murder may be undiscoverable.

It was not necessary to send Jem Pate warning: everything in that house of blood was arranged as if the visit of an expert detective were a matter of hourly expectation.

In the soft sunshine of the still afternoon, Marianne and her husband drove there together, and Severn was more than usually gay and kind as he lounged beside his wife, with her hand held caressingly in his.

But, in spite of her husband's nearness and dearness, and all the happiness that was so precious after past pain, Marianne felt her spirits damped as they alighted before the well-remembered door, and together entered the familiar garden.

In the serene autumn atmosphere the neglect everywhere apparent appealed strongly to the eye, mournfully to the heart; the seat inside the entrance was broken and half gone.

"Why let it all go to decay, Aleck?" said the wife, and she clung to his arm with a certain nervousness as they neared the house.

"Don't be superficial," he laughed. "The house is in excellent repair. Pate is steward, and sees to it all; and as to the garden, a little overgrowth may trouble your feminine eyes, but, rest assured, a couple of days' work would undo all the mischief there is there."

As their footsteps echoed along the paved verandah, the

library window opened as if in response, and there stepped forth a shrunken figure; bent and bowed as if with age, the face thin and lined, and surmounted by scanty locks of greyish hair, the eyes bleared and dim. It was a figure so expressive of age and suffering that Marianne pityingly wondered who it might be, till the man, recognising Severn, his whole countenance became infused with that dog-like devotion which only once before she had seen to marvel at in a human face. This was he—the youth whom she had seen with her husband under the acacias at the gate.

Pate made no effort to speak, but stood gazing from Severn to his companion with a slow questioning look. Marianne began to tremble.

"Oh, my dear," she whispered, "has he been ill? What has changed him?—he was a mere boy!" She *thought* more, but she could not express it, barely formulate it to herself.

In his gentle way Severn stepped forward, and laid his hand on the other's shoulder.

"This is my wife, Jem. She is concerned to see you so altered. She saw you by chance once before, it seems, and is prepared to make much of you, for the reason that she knows you are devoted to me."

Pate looked strangely at the well-dressed, tall, and handsome woman. Marianne's eyes were turned upon him with sweet compassion, and she put out her hand impulsively with a cordial gesture of pity and goodwill. The man noted the half-outstretched, delicate hand, though he made no effort to take it, and no detail of the lovely face or the fair, curling hair escaped him.

"You live here all alone," she began. "It must be dull—" Severn quietly stopped her.

"Pate cannot answer you," he said. "He is dumb. Pate, just go and open doors and windows, will you? My wife wants to go over the house."

Then, as the stooping figure turned in silence and disappeared with a peculiar, shambling gait, he continued, in a rapid, explanatory tone, "Poor fellow, his past is not altogether open to inspection, and a severe shock in connection with it, acting on wretched nerves, has made him what you see. I think the loss of speech is only temporary paralysis of the muscles, to put it without technicalities. At any rate, he's in good hands with me."

"Read? No, I don't think he can; yes, though, I have seen him spelling things over, but he can't write—wilfully forgot the little he was ever taught. He doesn't sleep here, has nice lodgings near, is rather timid over that odious affair happening so near." Marianne felt inexpressibly shocked. She could not forget the youth as she had seen him, and she accepted her husband's explanation without being relieved by it.

In silence, her spirits becoming more and more overcast, she followed Aleck from room to room, the figure of the strangely-afflicted youth that moved in front vaguely stirring the shadow of a forgotten dread she had hoped was not only asleep, but dead.

Everything in the house was in perfect order and repair: the comely housekeeper of by-gone days could not have observed more care; but Marianne only lingered for a short time in the room that had once been hers, and declined altogether to enter the apartment on the ground floor, where Aleck declared the innocent secret of the figure that had so frightened her on her last visit was to be found.

Instead, she hurried him back to the garden, more and more anxious with every moment to leave the place behind her—for ever.

On a garden chair in the verandah, as she swept along, she noticed a well-thumbed and dog-eared volume, and it struck her with a sort of strangeness that only came home long afterwards—in the way an impression can be received

unconsciously at the moment, and only recognised later—
that it was a scholastic and clearly printed edition of Shaks-
peare's "Macbeth."

Jem Pate stood waiting for them by the ruined seat, and
opened the door so as to conceal himself behind it.

"Good-bye, Jem," said Severn, with a cheery smile. "My
wife has quite demoralised me; but my researches are not
over yet, you know, and I shall be here again soon to keep
you company."

Pate only answered with a look, and Aleck passed gaily
on. Marianne lingered, her eyes full of pitying tears. She
was depressed, and this dumbness seemed so horrible, this
old age in youth so sad.

"I am so very sorry for you," she said. "I shall not forget
you, and if there is anything I can do for you, you must let
me know it." Pate's gaze wandered from the tender face to
the glittering rings of hair, and rested there till the dainty
vision was gone. The hair was in his mind as he turned
slowly back to the house, and the colour of it tinged his
thoughts.

Marianne shuddered violently as the carriage rolled
away down the quiet road.

"Someone walking over my grave," she said, lightly,
each turn of the wheels making her spirits rise. "Oh, Aleck,
to think we ever *lived* in such a dreary place: I never want
to go there again. You are quite welcome to keep it for
your horrid studies. By-the-bye, how does that poor fellow
express himself at all?"

"Oh, by signs chiefly; I understand him very well.
Besides, he can talk on his fingers rapidly when he likes. I
think, as I said before, it is only a matter of time, and speech
will come back to him."

"I wonder what will be the first word he will utter?" said
Marianne.

"I wonder," echoed Severn.

CHAPTER X.

AFTER this, the time passed peacefully away. Marianne was led down to the gates of doom through a pleasant land of flowers and joy; her husband was very tender with her, and her days were passed in sweet content.

The autumn had been distinguished by unusually fine weather, and the mellow glow of Indian summer lit up the shortening days till far into November; then came a change, and black fogs made one long night from dawn to dawn, and the melancholy overshadowing without seemed to darken the happy flow of the young wife's life. It was the commencement of the end.

With the beginning of December, the dismal weather still prevailing, Aleck began again to absent himself daily from his home, often not returning till the small hours of the morning. He made no attempt to conceal his movements from his wife, frankly owning that he paid his visits to their deserted residence, and that he was conducting experiments there of a daring and, as she would consider, doubtful nature, but still entirely in the interests of science and truth. "Would she like to accompany him once: had she the nerve to watch him at his work?"

Marianne remembered her jealous pangs of long ago, and hesitated, then shuddered at her own hesitation, and finally laughed with tremulous reproach, telling her husband that when his child was born she should expect science to lose its dreadful charm once and for ever. As for herself, she declared she wanted never to see the house in question again, and to forget, if she could, that she had so distasteful a rival in it.

And so the great Christian feast drew near.

* * * * * * * *

One night, about mid-way through the month, when the fog had lifted somewhat, and was only a rolling white mist, through which the lamps shone redly, and the few pedestrians moved giant-like, two women stood conversing at the corner of a quiet street in the Kilburn district.

The elder, a portly dame of about fifty, poorly dressed, but stamped with the respectability of honest toil, was listening with a mixture of disapproval and admiration to the animated talk of her companion. This was a much younger woman, scarcely more than a girl, but of remarkably fine development and good carriage. Her face, though somewhat spoiled by a too evident expression of self-assurance, was fresh and comely, bearing unmistakable traces of country birth; she emphasized her words with a good many tossings of the head, and seemed pleased at the impression she was making. Her dress was that of a respectable servant.

"Oh, you leave it to me, Mrs. Jenkins," she said, shaking her earrings; "it's all fair and square enough. An' don't you split, or it'll spoil all!"

"I'll not split," answered Jenkins. "It's nothin' to do with me; but you take care, Hannah. Many girls ha' thought as you do, and lived to curse themselves for bein' fools."

"He's different," said Hannah, with another toss. "He hoped from the first it would turn out as it has; he's like a gentleman for all he's rough, an' he'll make it worth my while to ha' listened to him."

"You're mighty confident," said Jenkins, with a disapproving snort. "Seems to me I'd ha' waited, an' made him marry me *fust*, not arterwards."

The young woman moved a little uneasily. "Oh, yes, now preach! Of course, I made a fuss, but—if you must have the whole of it——" Here she stooped forward, and whispered the end of her sentence into the other's ear.

Jenkins started, and stared. "Lawkes, now there's a man for you!" she ejaculated. "Well, now, what you ought to ha' done, Hannah Betsworth, would ha' been to box his ears soundly, and send him about his business. You're in a nice mess, I promise ye."

"Shut up!" Hannah was becoming angry. "I wish I'd never told ye; besides, you aint me, Mrs. Jenkins, an' its cruel of ye to worrit me at such a time. That's allus the way. Women is so spiteful when they hear of a better sweetheart than they ever had themselves."

The matron smiled in a lofty way. "Sweethearts that cal'clate like your'n does, aint much good to empty-headed gals; but, come, there aint no use in crying. Likely enough, he'll see ye through all right. What is he—p'leeceman?"

Indignation nipped Hannah's pettish sniffing in the bud.

"P'leeceman, indeed! No, thank ye, Mrs. Jenkins." And then the foolish creature, who could not have kept a still tongue in her head if another's life had been in question, much less when it concerned her own good name, proceeded volubly to explain that her follower was a seaman, that his moustaches curled like a pirate's, and his beard was brown and bushy, that whenever he was with her he treated her like a princess (only she didn't say princess: she used a term that conveyed more meaning to her hearer), and that he'd got a place of his own somewhere in the country where she was to go by and bye and keep a servant of her own. Jenkins shook her head. "Well, it's to be hoped the half of it'ull come true," she said "one thing's sure, you can't stay where you are much longer."

But Hannah was not listening; she had caught sight of a muffled figure looming thro' the fog, and knew it at once for the man she was waiting for. With a hasty word of adieu she stepped forward, and Mrs. Jenkins heard her eager exclamation of "John, I'm here," and caught a glimpse of the fellow's surly, bearded face as he turned roughly and caught the girl by the arm with an impatient growl.

Jenkins walked away feeling very moral. When young women like Hannah Betsworth go wrong, the least they can do is to hold their heads down about it and not take on airs, and if she were in the girl's place she should feel mighty uncomfortable about a sweetheart of Hannah's so-called "John's" kind.

But Hannah, herself, was troubled with no such misgivings. Although an exceedingly foolish, ignorant girl, whose head a very ordinary man would have had no difficulty in turning, she was conscious, without understanding why, that the man, whose notice her fine physique had attracted on her shopping errands, and who had won her with his doubtful devotions, was different to any "followers" she had ever expected to have, and it was this desire to brag of a conquest that in a vague way she felt to be quite different to what it appeared to be, that lead her to make indiscreet revelations to the honest charwoman who frequented her mistress's house. Indeed she was so foolish a girl that she was proud of the trouble she had fallen into, and, to do her justice, was so thoroughly infatuated with the man she knew as John Lewis that she was quite content to leave her future entirely in his hands, whether it included marriage or not.

John was a rough wooer. He never caressed, never spoke tenderly, scarcely even kindly to her, but all the same there was a consideration in his approach and manner that had much more of fascination in it for this uncouth servant-maid than any of the coarse gallantries a seaman might naturally offer.

"Who's that you were talking to?" demanded John, as they paced forward in the fog. Hannah told him.

"And what does she know about you and me?"

A lie sprang quickly to the girl's lips. "Law, John, nothin' 'cept that you an' me is sweethearting."

"Well, there is no need for concealment that I can see; I'll make an honest girl of you soon enough."

Hannah thought more of other things than her honesty, but she did not like to say so, so she giggled, and tossed her head, and hung heavily on to her companion's arm. His reflections were of a curious character.

"The first was a knave," John was thinking, "this is a fool; I do no great harm. Would you like to go to a theatre, my girl?" he asked aloud with sudden kindness in his voice. "Of course you would. Well, there aint any need to stick at shillings and pence as far as we are concerned. To-day week is your next night off, isn't it? Well, we'll go to a theatre then in grand style, and I'll send you some fine togs to sport in; that'll make your Mrs. Jenkins open her eyes and see I mean business."

Hannah's own eyes were open wide enough; she was gasping with almost painful delight. "But—but, John, what about gettin' back, mistress is very partic'lar; she never lets me out after nine?"

"You won't go back to your mistress that night, nor ever again afterwards," said John, with curious emphasis; "leave it to me Hannah; I've calculated everything to a nicety. Next Thursday you'll be mine once and for all, and I'll let the world know it. Now go home and be happy."

*   *   *   *   *   *   *   *

The days now left before the festival were to be remembered and talked of far into the New Year. For one thing, the fogs were appalling, and the "Doom of the great City" was in men's mouths once more; traffic was suspended, and business to a great extent had practically had to be abandoned, but the haunts of pleasure still nightly stood their ground and disgorged their hundreds into the street to fight their way home through the ghostly presence that filled the air as best they might, there being this encouragement, that the fogs lifted at night, and often between midnight and dawn cleared entirely away. A terrible railway catastrophe added to the gloom, and when at last "nor dim nor red, like God's own head," the sun shone once more on the troubled city, it beheld all classes stricken to the heart with horror at the cry of mutilation and murder once more in their midst.

Owing to her delicate health and the fact of her husband's continued and protracted absences, Marianne suffered acutely in the prevailing gloom; and a strange circumstance occurring at this time added alarm and bewilderment to a mind vainly trying to persuade itself that the glorious happiness of the past months was not vanishing behind the clouds of fresh sorrow and despair, like the sun behind the gloomy vapours without.

On the Monday preceding the frightful murder which afterwards transpired, the weather was comparatively clear, and the opportunity of walking or driving was eagerly seized by the well-to-do loungers in well-to-do homes who knew not the necessity of having to face the weather at all times.

Among others Marianne hailed with delight the round red ball that showed in the receding haze, and set off on foot to try and exorcise in the open air some of the misgivings that had begun to haunt her within doors. Returning an hour or two later, she was approaching her own door, when a figure whose stoop and shambling gait awoke painful memories, stepped from behind the shelter of a neighbouring portico and came rapidly towards her; it was the old, young man whom her husband called Jem, and whose dumbness seemed to her so strange and sad. With ready good will, though her heart was beating with half-fearful expectancy, Marianne stopped and extended her hand. She noticed, though scarcely with relief, that Severn treated the unfortunate well. Pate was comfortably, even fashionably, dressed, with an air of thoroughness and completeness that could only come from long use; but his face was stamped most woefully with disease and suffering, and his eyes were red and dim as those of some stricken woman; he raised them now, not to Marianne's face, but beyond it to her shining hair. Before she had time for more than a bare word of greeting, he had slipped something into her outstretched hand and was gone again, his shambling gait carrying him, as shambling gaits will, rapidly over the ground.

Marianne's first impulse was to follow and question him, then she remembered he could not speak. He had given her a sealed, but unaddressed, envelope. Turning it over, she entered the house pondering, and remained shut up in her own room some time before she found courage to do so simple a thing as break the fastening. "This weather is making a fool of me," she said at last, and tore the envelope open with an uneasy laugh. It contained a thumbed and soiled fragment of a page torn from a copy of Shakespere, and a sheet of thick note-paper on which something was inscribed that seemed at first sight nothing more than a succession of hieroglyphical marks, but which a close investigation discovered to be words, each letter of which had been laboriously copied from the printed type.

Marianne's heart beat more furiously: "Aleck thinks he cannot write," was her quick reflection. With infinite toil she spelt through the strange message. There were no stops, nor divisions of words, nor capitals, but at last she translated the long string of letters, thus: "e duz not no I can rite don't tell him ef it aint right you'll come."

It amounted to very little, but judging from the labour

it had cost him, Pate probably believed he had written a volume.

In fear and amazement Marianne stared from the letter to the page and from the page to the letter; she could make nothing of either; a fortnight before she would have taken both to her husband and asked an explanation; now, the cloud had settled down once again, and, although she knew it not, for the last time between them—she dared not.

It only needed a momentary second glance to show her that the page was torn from Macbeth, and instantly she remembered the thumbed copy she had seen on the verandah of that fateful house; but the puzzle of its presence there was no clearer. She read the lines again and again, she searched her mind all the evening and half the night through for some explanation—in vain. But her mind could not let the mystery go; it busied itself with it feverishly, and while still working half-unconsciously, suddenly, in a moment, with the certainty of inspiration, the force of revelation, light was there.

*   *   *   *   *   *   *   *

It seemed as if John Lewis wished to give as much publicity as possible to the fact that he was taking his lowly sweetheart to the theatre in a style befitting his independent spirit and his well-filled pockets. The week of expectation was passed by Hannah Betsworth in a state of such exulting delight as two such lives as she might ordinarily have expected to look forward to, could not have given her in their whole course.

She talked to Jenkins volubly, and that saved her from the effects of suppressed excitement; she sang over her work and laughed aloud in glee when her mistress told her she was looking blooming, and that she thought the milkman fancied her. When the promised finery arrived, addressed to Miss Betsworth, and brought by a private messenger, the girl nearly died with joy; even the distrustful and disapproving Jenkins was carried away by the sight of feminine adornments such as even the small tradesmen's wives who employed her only sighed for and never possessed.

"Well, he thinks a heap of you," she said, "an' I only hopes, Hannah, you won't forget old friends who have given you good advice, when you're set up for life."

Hannah's promises were wild; she thought herself the most fortunate woman in the world.

Accompanying the handsome clothes was a note written in a clear round hand, and signed "John Lewis"; it set forth that Hannah was on no account to say anything to her mistress, but to leave everything to him, and that to avoid any questions he had made arrangements with the barmaid of a small public-house, and who was also daughter of the proprietor and well-known to him, that on the eventful evening Hannah should arrange her toilet there. He named the exact moment at which he would meet her, fog or no fog, and begged her to be punctual.

Punctual! Fully an hour before the appointed time, Hannah was ready, and awaiting John's arrival with a feverish excitement that glowed in each cheek and eye, and added a final touch to the really fine appearance she presented. Her elegant attire seemed chosen with a sense of fitness seamen do not often possess. Jenkins and the barmaid were loud in admiration, and even Lewis himself, when, later on, he led his charge out to the vehicle in waiting, seemed proud of the admiration she excited, and lingered with her under the full glare of the lamps, uttering a word or two of warmer praise than she had ever heard from his lips. Those who saw the couple were not likely to forget them, nor did they.

At the theatre it was the same; their seats were in a

conspicuous part of the house, and the man's object seemed rather to attract than ward off attention. Ecstasy and diffidence had rendered the girl speechless; her cheek flushed and paled, her eyes glowed, dilated wide, and her fine figure and unusual bearing riveted the notice of many who in a few short hours had terrible cause to remember both the handsome young woman and the surly-looking bearded fellow by her side.

Leaving the house before the performance was nearly over, Lewis muffled his face in a thick wrapper and bade the girl put on her veil. She was so completely dazed that her conduct was irreproachable. They drove rapidly, the night being comparatively clear, and in a northerly direction, but, while there was still time to have branched off to a hundred places, the driver was peremptorily stopped and the two alighted and walked quietly away arm-in-arm.

CHAPTER XI.

AGAIN the same picture, the great leaping fire and the comfortable room; the intense heat and the sleeping woman.

Hannah had been plied with wine and lay inert in the same low chair where the other victim's yellow head had rested. Severn had soothed her into slumber with his devil's kiss, and now, his clever disguise abandoned, stood over her in his normal habit, and with gentle melancholy on his face, mused as the thermometer rose.

He was alone; there was not a sound within or from without, but yet the silence spoke: "Hush! Murder! Murder!" . . .

The noiseless timepiece pointed to the hour of one, and Severn bent low over the sleeper. Exclaiming at the strange heat, she had loosened the fastenings of her dress ere becoming unconscious, and her full throat was bare as she lay with her handsome head thrown back. The man stooped and gently kissed it; he thought she would feel the coming blow as little as the kiss, but, without warning, in an instant the closed lids flew up and life leapt back into the woman's eyes. Startled by the suddenness of it, Severn drew back; the girl sprang to a sitting posture, and then wildly to her feet: she gave one wide glance of terror from the man's white face to the shining things upon the table; sharpened by panic her wits guessed at the truth. There was time for one look round, then, as Severn's lithe arms gripped her, time for one short, sharp scream that pierced through bolts and bars to die unheeded in the air.

Crazy with terror, the wretched girl opened her lips to cry again, but the murderer deftly thrust his handkerchief between her jaws, pinioning then her hands; but Hannah was tall and powerfully built, and mortal fear toughened the sinews. With eyes that started from their sockets and hair bristling from her head she tried to free herself; and only with tremendous exertion could Severn hold his ground. Unspeakably awful was the silence of the struggle. He called for no aid; she *could* not. Her dress was torn from her back, the blood began to ooze from her roughened wrists, her face grew purple with each effort to draw the gasping breath through the widely-opened nostrils. From Aleck's face the sweat poured like water, but his set features never moved; a something that was neither of beast nor of devil gleamed in his eyes as he turned them now and again on the silent clock. Round and round in a hideous embrace the two swayed and turned; the woman's hair swung behind her almost to her knees; presently a convulsion passed over the distorted face, her efforts slackened, grew spasmodic, ceased, were still. Raising her head as it fell back, she cast one awful look upon the Thing that held her, then shuddered strongly, and tumbled prone upon the floor.

She was not dead. Severn did not need to bend the knee beside her to see that; as easy to recall her life as to take it from her. It was a strange moment for hesitation, yet, as he knelt there, he debated within himself, and was inclined almost to pity and restore her, the lines of his mouth relaxed into their usual grieving, childlike droop, he laid one hand as if in tenderness on her brow, then a jibe came to his ear and a touch to his elbow, he smiled at himself, and—cut her throat.

*   *   *   *   *   *   *   *   *

Marianne's rose-hung boudoir was a picture of comfort this frosty, December evening; the fog had disappeared and the day been cheered by pale winter sunshine, that, make-believe as it was, did good to the heart and eyes of all.

The lady sat alone, sipping tea, and toasting her daintily-slippered feet before the brilliant fire; her *négligé* gown became her beauty, and the shaded lustre of the reading-lamp enhanced the charm. There, in her rich robe, in her rich room, with all the adjuncts of luxury about her, she looked what she was *not*—the embodiment of a fortune-blessed and happy woman. Happiness seemed again to be evading Aleck's wife; Jem Pate's letter rankled in her mind; she could not dismiss it, she could make nothing of it.

Presently, as she lounged there brooding, the cry of a newspaper boy in the street below aroused her attention: the sound was unusual. She listened, moved to the window, and listened again. "Horrible murder in the North of London; second woman mutilated; police on the track." She gathered so much from the disjointed yells of the boy, then impulsively rang her bell and bade them buy and bring her a paper—"one of the special editions being cried at that moment in the street."

The maid was a little surprised at the order, and noticed the white, stricken face with which her mistress took the copy; she commented on it to her fellow-servants, and remembered it to her sorrow afterwards.

Reseating herself, Marianne turned up the lamp, and proceeded with a good deal of deliberation to unfold the paper and find the account of the murder. Yes. There it was. The horrid headlines seemed to stare at her with personal meaning, but she read on steadily while Jem Pate's letter and the torn page from Macbeth obtruded themselves against her will between every word of the paragraph.

"Early this (Friday) morning, the dead and frightfully mutilated body of a young woman was discovered on almost the identical spot where the unfortunate Polly Dean was found little more than a twelve-month ago."

Then followed the points of similarity between the two atrocities.

"The corpse," it added, "was only partially clad, but was that of an unusually tall and well-developed woman, since identified by many as having been seen the preceding evening in conspicuous company with a man fully described as under."

So much was the bare gist of it. The whole, it was stated, made a story without parallel in the annals of crime; suspicion pointing strongly to the surly seaman who had been the young servant's escort to the theatre.

Marianne sat on thinking, thinking, with a face of stone. At last she reached out her hand, and from a heap of papers near her lifted the torn page from Macbeth. It contained a portion of the scene between Macbeth and Macduff, where the regicide exultingly defies his adversary that is of "woman born," and Macduff, answering, bids his "charm despair," and tells him why.

She read the lines as she had read the report in the newspaper, with a curious deliberation. At last she understood their inference, and with the unalterable conviction of understanding it aright.

No sound came from her or motion, save that once she shivered slightly. In time her figure seemed to stiffen, and her face gradually to assume the hue and rigidity of death.

The little dial on the mantelshelf, swinging in the hands of a Sèvres Cupid, chimed the hour of six like the silver bells swaying in the breeze of Mistress Mary's garden, and at the same moment the door opened softly upon Severn himself. He was in evening dress and wore a white flower, his look was distinguished and refined, his appearance altogether desirable in the eyes of one to whom he might be dear. Stepping noiselessly across the thickly-carpeted floor, he bent over his wife's chair with a caressing gesture and a gently uttered word of love. Then his eyes fell on her face ... Slowly and awfully the change crept over his own. Stealthily as a cat he crept round the chair, and, leaning against the mantel, gazed statue-wise with gloomy eyes and grieving mouth at the corpse-like figure stretched before him. But Marianne was not yet dead. Slowly and awfully she lifted her eyes; slowly and awfully, as rigidly as if wrapt in a shroud, she rose to her full height.

"You have killed me," she said, in a strange and hollow voice. "Tell me, now that I am dead, shall you mutilate *me*?"

The man seemed suddenly to break loose from a spell.

"There is no need," he cried; "it is accomplished; it is done! Marianne! wife! beloved, hear me, I implore!"

But, moving like a ghost, she evaded him, and stepped backwards towards the window. Her face was like the face of one who has long been dead.

"There *shall* be no need," she whispered, stooping towards him while the lips for an instant revealed the teeth in a ghastly smile—then—the keen air blew in upon him through the opened window like the stroke of a sword. He heard a strange sound—a very strange sound, then shriek on shriek. Smiling curiously to himself, Severn sat on in a red-flecked darkness—curiously still.

*   *   *   *   *   *   *   *

"You'd no bizness to ha' giv' her the paper," sobbed the cook, "an' she as she was? 'twas that as druv' her to it, take my word."

"That's right, blame me," shrieked the wretched maid, prostrate with hysterics. "As if I could know it 'ud turn her brain. Oh, Lord, I wish I was dead before ever I'd lived to see such a sight!"

"The Judgment day ain't far off," said Jenkins, whose teeth were chattering; "but you might ha' had more sense, Christine, when you seed her so scared; being as she was, she feared someone might use her—"

"Don't talk of it," yelled the women, and Christine screamed again and hid her face.

"What's master doing now?" quoth the awestruck footman.

"Someone's with him," answered the butler, wiping his kindly eyes. "He may come round, but it's my belief he's gone stark, starin' mad. The Lord have mercy upon this house."

"Amen," groaned his auditors in a miserable chorus.

CHAPTER XII.

MARIANNE SEVERN'S tragic death was easily and plausibly accounted for; and the crime which had had this stupendous effect upon the suicide was thereby terribly impressed upon men's minds. The dead woman's stricken friends and neighbours felt as if it were a personal matter, that the miscreant, the recital of whose deeds had sent this gentle spirit, crazed with fear, stark out of existence, should be brought to justice. Every effort that public endeavour could make, and private incentive induce, was put forth in pursuit of the murderer. The murderer, mark you, was bearded, surly, beetle-browed, seafaring in look and manner, and had committed the murder within a certain radius, within a certain time. His name was known to the police. The victim's relationship to him was ascertained beyond a doubt; the motive of the crime seemed apparent; the fact that it was premeditated was evident. Yet with all this, and much more in hand, inquiry at last died away for sheer want of material to work upon.

Marianne Severn and the murdered servant were buried on the same day. The two funerals, so allied, and yet so distinctive, attracted an immense amount of attention. Severn stood bare-headed by his wife's grave, while a sober-faced man held him tightly by the arm. "A mad doctor," whispered the crowd, and hinted that after this the bereaved husband's career would be in other hands than his own.

True and unalterable grief evinces a species of greatness in the mourner; for the ordinary mind is incapable of protracted sorrow. Severn's friends, recognising this capacity in him, respected him for it, and they who were the nearest to him declared that it was sorrow pure and simple, and that he was greatly in need of moral support, and worthy deep and universal pity. Some few there were who commented curiously on the fact that Severn's name had been brought into prominence in connection with both the appalling murders that had stained the year. They deduced nothing from the circumstance; they only spoke of it as strange. The majority, however, merely recognised a fearfully-stricken man, whose popularity and good reputation had not availed to save him from what could scarcely have overtaken him more direfully had heredity declared itself.

But time softened the keen edge of even this second horror. The new year opened bright and fair, and both the murdered and suicide were forgotten, save that it still now and again passed uneasily across the public mind that such a murderer was still undetected in their midst.

To the surprise of some who had expected from him they knew not what, after the first prostration, Severn rather avoided than sought the isolation that would have seemed most compatible with the intense distress no one could doubt he was a prey to.

True, he broke up his establishment and removed from the stately home where Marianne had lived, to luxuriant bachelor apartments; but instead of dismissing either the more sober-minded of his friends or the lighter companions of elegant dissipation, he gathered them more closely about him, and lavished his wealth freely in incessant, sometimes doubtful, distractions. This state of things degenerated in time into debauch.

At first Severn's excesses were tolerated by excusing friends, as a not unusual attempt to get rid of the canker-worm of intolerable grief; and, before this charitable construction had perforce to altogether give way to a verdict that was not so lenient, a new freak seized the widower.

First settling all his mundane affairs with admirable exactitude, Severn, after wild, farewell orgies, retired suddenly and completely from the haunts that had known him. His chief friends had begun to be of those who do not trouble much about the absent; and it was some time before it was discovered that he had sought the old seclusion and loneliness of the detached house in the northern suburb. From this retreat all the machinations of spendthrifts and fair, frail ones failed to draw him, and better meaning ones did not try. The weeks rolled into months, the months into a year, and when a third Christmas brought back to some a faint and shuddering memory of that time of gloom and death and murder, Aleck Severn was found to be gone even from that desolate refuge. Not a trace of his whereabouts had been left, and the casual enquiries that were ever set on foot utterly failed to discover whether he was dead or living, or where, or how.

"A pity," people said, and shrugged their shoulders. "Something wrong somewhere. A good life spoilt."

Then Aleck Severn was forgotten; the murders were as though they had never been; the costly wreaths withered and were not replaced on Marianne's grave.

CHAPTER XIII.

A LONG alternation of night and day, and sleeping and waking—and see, fifteen years, as men reckon time, have passed!

In the golden glow of a midsummer sun two men paced slowly along the broad *chaussée* which, skirted on one side by a deep and mossy moat, embraced like a broad, white girdle the green and fountained gardens of a quiet German town. On the garden side of the walk, the trees, interspersed with the odorous linden, were wide and umbrageous; but the two companions avoided any space of shadow, and crept along in the full glare of the sun.

They had the promenade to themselves—no native walked abroad at such hours and in such heat; but these men were not natives. The low tone of the one voice alone audible, though they appeared to be conversing earnestly together, was English, and the faces, turned up every now and then full to the scorching rays, had little of the lymphatic Teuton in either.

Reaching a seat which, from its exposed position, most people in their senses would have avoided, the two seated themselves, and for a time seemed content to bask silently in the sun, writhing in a strange enjoyment of the heat.

"Fifteen years ago!" said the one presently, and heaved a long sigh. "Fifteen years ago!" There was no need to soften the tone—the voice could stir no long-forgotten memories in chance hearers. Here Aleck Severn could air his reminiscences unquestioned and unknown.

Severn had greatly changed. The years that, under different auspices, should have but mellowed him into the prime of a fine manhood, had left him now, at little more than fifty, an old, old man, and the soft brown hair that, though thinned and unkempt, had still retained its pleasant colour, as brown hair often will, was curiously at variance with the wrinkled, withered face beneath, where the always deep-set eyes had sunk still further into cavernous sockets, shining with a look in which melancholy was touched with fear. The once sensitive mouth was gathered now into a senile leer. In form the man was bent and shrunken, and the hands that grasped the knotted stick he leant upon had lost all suppleness and shapeliness and the warm colouring of youth.

Time had told less markedly upon the murderer's companion. Jem Pate had been faithful to his master with an exceeding devotion, and, though lost youth had never returned to him, and the long locks that fell to his shoulder were white as snow, and the wasted frame and the shambling gait were still there, the look of mortal disease was gone, while the pale blue eyes had lost some of their wistfulness. Mingling, moreover, with the intense sadness of the thin face was an air of almost peaceful serenity, contrasting favourably with the gloomy and devilish disappointment stamped on every line of Severn's altered face.

If, indeed, our sins are our *Motives*, this outcast wretch, Jem Pate, might one day, going to his own place, find mercy at the hands of an unknown God.

For fifteen years he had been silent—wilfully so. Such was Severn's unalterable opinion. He pronounced it openly and frankly, and had for long tried many means of entrapping the man into sudden self-confession—so far, in vain. Not even the experiments of the one or two authorities whose aid Aleck could not resist bringing in, had effected anything whatsoever; and, though the doubt still remained and was often expressed in Pate's very ears, his affliction was either very real or his self-control very great. From the night when the sight of the woman's yellow hair had frosted his own for ever, Pate's lips had been sealed as if with the finger of death itself.

This silence had not, as might have been expected, communicated itself to Aleck Severn. Rather, the one-sidedness of his talk had made him garrulous, and, though communication between the two was a rapid and easy matter, the intercourse was generally of the nature of a monologue, to which the dumb man responded with his dimmed but expressive glance.

"I like this," muttered Severn, twining basilisk-fashion in the heat. The desire for intense warmth, common to both of the men, was abnormal, and not to be explained in any ordinary way. It seemed the outcome of some unhal-lowed chill in the blood.

After a time, further mutterings became connective, and the monologue went on in a louder tone.

"I wish you would sometimes answer me, Jem. I know you could if you liked. It is all folly. Why are you silent? I have been very kind to you—you know it. That second time I did not call you, I fought it out all alone. It was because I loved you, Jem. I did not want to prove that you would fail me. Then we should have had to part. I would not try your faithfulness too far.

"Perhaps you think you have nothing to thank me for, and that if I had left you alone you would have been used to damnation by this time; but you're wrong. I've done a good thing for you by letting you love me. You do love me, Jem Pate. Yes, I know you do. Then why don't you speak to me? There wouldn't be so much of other jabbering in my ears if you would only talk."

Then the querulous, plaintive tone changed; the speak-er's head fell forward on his breast. It was evident that he was now merely thinking aloud.

"Fifteen years ago! She would have been a stately matron now, and her child would be almost a man. Marianne was not of the stuff that mothers girls. I wonder if she knows. I wonder what she thinks of it. It was a pity: so much exquisite skill quite thrown away. If she knows anything she must know that, and be sorry for me.

"After all, it was evenly balanced—I made her most supremely happy. With another man she might have lived to be a hundred; but a hundred years could not have contained so much joy as I gave her in one month. It was the same with each of them. They found their happiness in *me*, and they had as much of it as they could bear. I did them more good than ill. Life is so easily given—so easily taken away, that it is a thing of far more consequence to have shown three people—three women, Jem—how delicious life can be, than either to give it or take it away. Eh, Jem, you know that is so, don't you?"

This train of thought was not new to the listener. He was acquainted with all Severn's sophistries, though scarcely in his own soul did he know how much he believed in them.

The philosopher never asked his companion to justify the crimes he had abetted; but he justified them daily to himself—not so much in any spirit of remorse, as from a species of diabolical pride. He wished to keep it always clearly reasoned out before his own and Jem's mind that his blood-shedding was not like any other. The end he had in view had been *life*, not death; and if murder remained the only means to obtain that end, he had made more than ample compensation to his victims by compressing into one short epoch more than all the value the possession of life could have possibly held for them, even if extended over a long number of years.

"You know that, don't you, Jem?" he repeated, and Jem gave him one of his strange glances by way of reply.

Then Severn maundered on, leaning heavily on his stick. He spoke continually of his dead wife. There seemed no such thing as present or future in his reflection; and in unbroken silence the one listened while the other prated of the nameless horrors of the past.

The two lingered in the *chaussée* through all the noon-tide, now sitting basking, now creeping slowly from one bench to another. At length, as the heat lessened, and merry voices began to be heard in the gardens, and the rattle of hoofs on the road beyond the moat—general signs that the town was rousing itself, and coming out to enjoy the day—they turned themselves about, and, proceeding at such a snail's pace that the sun was low in the heavens ere they reached the end of their walk, passed through the quiet streets out into a country road beyond.

"I think those are two such dear old men," said one school-girl to another, idly swinging her satchel as she watched them pass. "They seem to be so fond of one another. I like to see men so."

"Well, *I* don't," declared her companion. "Heinrich says it's not natural, and that good men are never so attached. What isn't natural isn't good, he says, and, do you know, he believes those men aren't old at all, but young, and that they keep a beautiful princess shut up in that old house of theirs. Heinrich says he's seen her, and that it's a horrid shame."

Girl number one, on whose mind no Heinrich had been working, scouted the idea. Heinrich and his sister were narrow-minded, she affirmed, and slandered the men because they were foreigners, and never drank too much beer. She was not old enough to philosophise, and therefore could not argue out to herself that, as a rule, it is the tremendous truths that spring from the seed of a little mistake.

This girlish criticism may not have been the only one passed on the two Englishmen; but if they excited remark they were unconscious of it. Quite unmolested, merely exchanging a civil greeting here and there, they directed their steps to a small, detached cottage, very humble in appearance, but possessing a pleasant garden, well stocked with trees, and surrounded by a stout and unusually high wooden fence.

The western sun was flooding the place with genial colour, and, with its white walls and bright shutters, the little retreat amid fine trees looked a far from undesirable home for weary feet. But, as they neared the gate, the evil, which had taken the place of bygone melancholy in Aleck Severn's face, deepened and darkened. He leant heavily on his companion's arm, and his slow steps lagged still more, while his eyes searched each casement as the cottage came into view. With ill-concealed dread, he shrank at the rustling in the branches, and peered into the corners, as Pate raised the latch, with the air of a man who fears an unwelcome, yet unlikely sight. Utter loathing and abhorrence was in the tone with which he turned to his fellow.

"Keep it away to-night, Jem," he whispered. "For God's—— in the Devil's name keep it away."

Pate felt how he shuddered, and touched his arm reassuringly. The little scene had been enacted too often to be dwelt on.

On his own face was a strange light. There was rather eagerness than horror in his gaze. He quickened his shambling gait, and something almost like a smile touched his silent lips.

"You hear me?" gasped Severn, as they stood at length in the barely-furnished hall. "There it is, coming already. Keep it away, or I will kill you both."

This threat had probably lost its force through repetition. It fell on unheeding ears. Pate did not even turn as his master disappeared, but stood with his eyes fixed on the stairway, on which a curious footfall sounded. Whatever his thoughts may have been, it was plainly to be read on that expectant face that Aleck Severn did not own them all.

CHAPTER XIV.

THE Heinrich of the school-girls' conversation was a beardless student, whose blonde hair fell about his neck, surmounted by a tiny white-banded cap, and who, in cold weather, did not disdain to wrap his noble shoulders in a green plaid shawl, folded squarewise, nor to protect his woollen-cased fingers from frost-bites in a substantial muff.

The romance of the "beautiful princess," and the Mephistophelian characteristics of the two Englishmen, confided to his adoring sister, had originated in the following manner:

To the back of the cottage which Severn occupied, and separated from it only by a stretch of meadow-land, the town, in a fit of somewhat aimless enterprise, had reared a large brick building, the ultimate destiny of which, even when completed, was some time in being decided. Meanwhile, during the discussion of the respective merits of library, museum, seminary, gymnasium, musical college—for each and any of which purposes an institution was highly desirable—the lofty lower rooms of the new building were devoted to a series of evening lectures on popular subjects, the classes being crowded by that large element to be found in every German community, which has for its principal object universal and illimitable self-improvement.

Among the spectacled and long-haired youths who thronged in garments of quaint cut to acquire knowledge that would be general in, perhaps, a generation to come, was our friend Heinrich. Heinrich, having the whole distance of the town to travel, and his legs not being of the strongest, cast about in his mind for a means of abridging the weary tramp to and fro. He was not long at arriving at a conclusion, based on abstruse scientific deduction, that, by crossing the meadow tract, and gaining thereby the road that lay beyond, he should shorten his way by a good English mile. To cross the meadow was easy, and, though a broad belt of private property, devoted to various purposes, even now separated him from the highway, it was not long before his theoretical basis found a practical demonstration in the form of a six inch wide strip of grass, which, shelving on one side into a deep ditch, ran along at the foot of the high wooden palings of one of the scattered rustic dwellings which fronted the road, and formed an isthmus-like communication (for the ground on either side might have been water for all the good it was) between the Seminary at the one end and Heinrich's home at the other.

Having to walk across this isthmus, as much like a goat, though without its grace as he was able, and not wishing to attract untoward attention, the student confined his use of the meadow-way till the return journeys when passengers along the road were few and far between. To his right as he chamois'd along, was the unpleasant ditch, beyond it the deserted, but still guarded, surroundings of a decaying art school; to his left the wooden palings of the Englishmen's cottage. By standing on tiptoe, and craning his neck, he could, with discomfort, see over into the dusky garden; and it became his habit to take one such peep on each of his tri-weekly pilgrimages.

The result of these observations was vague, but he thought they warranted him in making the certain disclosures to his sister which she improved upon as occasion directed.

He himself was prepared with a logical and unanswerable apology should the Englishman one day perchance emerge from his castle, and resent the intrusion of his hat-brim, his spectacles and his protuberant eyes.

But the same autumn winds that blew down the leafy screen that surrounded the house, and opened up a wider area of observation, flooded the meadow and the ditch with rain and reduced the strip of grass to an impassable bog. Heinrich was obliged to abandon his new route and return to the orthodox track, and Jem Pate shuffling along through the fallen leaves and shivering in his pile of wraps looked round, thankful for their isolation, and little knew from what dangerous observation the dwelling and its occupants had been temporarily saved.

After the wind and the rain came the silent snow; and when it had fallen for days, old winter took the German land and bound the white robes he loved about her with girdles of frost, till she looked to him like the Snow Princess in Andersen's fairy-tale, and he kissed her again and again till everybody shivered and said how cold it was, and the "Christ-kind" stood in the windows wrapped in a snow-mantle, and with icicles for a crown.

As the white festival drew near, the old horror of the season and the grip of the cold settled, as it always did, only this year with greater intensity, upon the household in the suburban cottage.

This was their first winter in the German town. In the preceding spring some strange whim had brought Severn back to Europe from the northern shores of Africa, and after wandering from place to place, he had finally seen and secured this quiet retreat.

It reminded him somewhat of his old home in the sub-urbs of the English capital. The heat of the Algerian sun truly had been pleasant, but it pleased him, too, to think of building up one of those huge fires again, and, sitting before it, go over in fancy those scenes of the past. It had always been the case with him, that nothing that appealed solely through the imagination could daunt or could win him; what the *mind* could bring before Aleck Severn, of the deeds he had done, though vivid and ghastly, did not appal him a whit. But he was not without his Nemesis. There was a tangible and bodily terror at the murderer's elbow that had nothing to do with reverie.

It was the night before Christmas and glittering with frost. The stars shone like stars only do, when children carol to them in the snow; the air was full of an eloquent and profound stillness, yet far along the country roads a benighted wanderer might have caught the sound of distant laugh and song.

In his wayside cottage, Aleck Severn sat alone, before a fire of wood, burning fiercely in the open grate of a huge white stove; he looked very old as he leant forward on a stick, and gazed with cavernous eyes deep into the white hot embers.

"It has not been worth it," he muttered—"not been worth it. When they read my story someone else will grasp at my idea, and perfect it, and hand it down to fame, while I, perchance, shall be only execrated and defamed. It is no use to be the originator of ugliness; one must create beauty, and then men say: 'See, the end justifies the means.' And yet, the great secret was almost in my grasp, I missed it by the breadth of a hair, the tick of a clock. Life is voluntary movement, given all the accessories, produce voluntary movement and you have life.

"I have produced it—but not beautiful life. That is for someone more fortunate to attain to. A beautiful life that shall be perpetuated for ever; perpetual movement, perpetual life; such a life is worth the value we others put on our ignoble days. There must be a reason for this disproportion between value and creation. I have tried to *catch* life, and succeeded only to fail—to *fail!* Well, the end is not far off, and in hell I will tear the secret from my mother's vitals. There *is* no hell! Could such a thing as *she* transmit *immortality?* No, I was a fool to give up so soon, I should have tried again and again."

Ah! Severn broke off suddenly, and, raising his devil's face, seemed to listen with dread intentness; no sound, nor moan of wind, nor fall of foot.

He rose noiselessly and moved half-way to the closed door, then stopped, and returning to the fire, heaped on more wood with elaborate noise; the flames roared, the sparks flew; every space of the small darkly-panelled room was ruddily illumined.

"She will know I am not asleep," he muttered, and sat down again with his glance fixed horridly on the door. The minutes passed. Whatever it was that the man had heard, it was not repeated, and gradually he fell again into a deep and deeper reverie, while the flames sank down unheeded, and the faggots fell into heaps of livid ash.

Far into the night, the door unclosed, and Pate, with his shambling gait, stole into the room. He seemed to have just entered the house—there was snow on his boots and rime on his hair; his face was white, and pinched, and chilled, but his dim eyes seemed rekindled; there was a light in them like the faint reflection of one of the sparkling stars overhead.

Seeing that his master slept or was so sunk in trance-like thought as not to be aware of his presence, he stayed but to place fresh fuel on the dying embers, and then, as noise-lessly as he had come, departed, like a moving spectre that might be part of the dreamer's visions . . . .

CHAPTER XV.

ON the upper floor, in a plainly but comfortably furnished chamber, another wood fire was burning, too, far into that Xmas night, and over it there crouched a strange and woeful being. The window was uncurtained, and the stars shone in brightly through the top of the fire-reddened panes, and the sheets of snow stretching away below filled the night with a glistening white radiance.

The face, or figure, if face it had, if figure it were, was hidden, the shape almost entirely concealed by a garment of uncouth fashion and flowing form.

Dark hair fell unrestrained over neck and shoulders, as only women's hair generally is allowed to fall, but, further, there was nothing distinctive of sex or age in the thing that was huddled, as if in anguish, on the hearth—anguish—for there could be no touch of cold in that gently-tempered atmosphere. About the whole apparition was something that would have prevented a casual observer from caring to enquire too closely into its characteristics.

"It." Horrible! Human, and yet—"It.". . .

The faint creaking made by a softly-shambling step mounting the stairs roused the huddled shape; and a half-face was turned to the door, as it was cautiously tried, and then opened, by Jem Pate. It was the profile of a woman and of unique, unearthly beauty. The man came forward to the fire, and knelt down lowly, as if in reverence or prayer; then, with gently shining eyes, drew the hair-crowned head to his shoulder and murmured tender lullabies that could never have issued from the lips of the dumb. The woman, if woman she were, made no resistance and gave no sign, but presently she slept, or seemed to sleep, as if she had but awaited him. Jem Pate looked down, and shuddered; then, with an awful tenderness, lightly threw a covering over the sight, now fully revealed as the head rested against his shoulder.

And so, in haunted watchfulness for the two, and in woful slumber for the one, the night passed and the dawn rose blood-red upon the Holy Festival.

It was the jocund chiming of the Xmas bells that woke the madman. Woke! It did not seem to Severn that he ever slept, his nights were but a continuation of his daylight dreams, unencumbered by the interruptions of the flesh. He sat through the dark hours in the same position and in the same chair he occupied by day, and with the first signs of daylight generally sought his room, where he remained shut up till far into the morning.

Food, cheery meals, happy intercourse and domestic comfort of any sort or kind, seemed things impossibly incongruous in the midst of this unblessed household; yet, whatever their nocturnal habits and their memories and their future, day by day they ate and drank much as others do. There was no need of stint in the internal economy of the cottage, and if the furniture was plain and the fare frugal it was because Jem Pate, who managed such things entirely, was limited in his notions, and Severn had not troubled to widen them. Aleck had long since converted all his possessions into gold. The money was in various chests, and Pate helped himself as he wanted.

The merry clanging of the bells filled the still air till noon-tide. At the same hour a plain, neatly-laid luncheon awaited Severn, and Pate knocked softly at the door to summon him.

Aleck responded with unusual alacrity, and the dim but quick eyes of the servitor noticed instantly that a change had passed over him. He was dressed with care; there was some return of elasticity in his gait, and the soft brown hair arranged with a remembrance of bygone pride, did not seem to-day so absurdly out of place above the face beneath, for the look of evil was submerged in the rejuvenating radiance of long vanished hopes. Briskly sitting down at table, Severn dined with an air of pleasure, then called the companion of his exile to his side.

Pate's eyes rested on him with their doglike devotion, but there was watchfulness in them. *He*, himself, was with his master: his thoughts guarded the shape upstairs.

"Jem," said Severn, and his tone was fresh, "I hold that man or woman very foolish who, having some priceless pearls, well strung, should in a rash experiment, foolishly stretch the string beyond necessary endurance. It breaks, and the pearls are lost.

"We *know* that everything has its limits; to try to *prove* it must end in loss. Fifteen years ago I forbore to test you; you were very faithful, very beholden to me, and I did not wish to tax you beyond your limits, and so lose you.

"That woman nearly mastered me; she had *dark* hair, Jem, not yellow, but still I would not call you. I did not want to *prove* that you would not come: in my heart I knew it.

"Now, again, I will not test you too far; I will spare you, because it is a pity to spoil such faithfulness as yours, and in secret already, I *know* that you have chosen between us, between me and that thing upstairs. Now, hark, the same house cannot longer hold the two of us. It terrifies me into imbecility, its hideousness appals me; its great eyes reproach me with the cruelty of failure.

".... During my thoughts last night, much was revealed to me: I have confounded mysteries, I have been a fool. Men are but the receptacle through which the stream of mystery flows from its beginning to its end. It is movement during its stay; it flows on, and movement stops. I thought, vain wretch, that to discover movement would be to discover life; I looked for the effect in the cause; the mystery pursued its way, I only marred the receptacle.

"Now I have another scheme, one worthier of a thinking man. I will prepare the receptacle, not destroy the movement; it shall be beautiful as a dream, and then, when it is ready, *I* will die to give it life.

"Ah, I have a glorious hope: this is '*to be*' for ever."

Carried away by his wild new visions, Severn had forgotten his first object in speaking, and forgotten that he was not alone. He had risen from his chair, his arms extended, his face aglow, and his figure drawn up to its full height once more. The sluggish apathy, the evil dreams of the fifteen years were gone, and in his newly-born enthusiasm Aleck Severn looked again like the well-favoured youth, at whose knees the maid who loved him had pleaded in an autumn garden years ago.

A sound from without the room recalled him, it was the curious footfall to be heard sometimes on the stairs of that quiet home. Severn turned to his silent companion, visibly shrinking and paling.

"You are not letting it come here?" he cried in fearful accents. Pate shook his head; his look was indescribable; he loved his master, but he loved, with that strange soul of his, his master's victim more.

The footstep ceased, but the interruption had disturbed Aleck's mood. Pouring out a bumper of the light wine of the country that stood on the table, he left his seat, and coming up to the dumb man laid one hand upon his shoulder in the way he had been wont; with the other he held the brimming glass; his back was directly to the door; Jem faced it, and his eyes were fastened on it. Severn seemed at a rebound to go back to the freshness and vigour of manhood, the other grew older with every moment, and bowed as if under an insupportable burden.

"Drink to our parting, Jem; I will not let you make your choice, for you *have* chosen, and you yourself shall not pronounce yourself unfaithful. Half that is in this house is yours; take it and go—*with It*. Ah, traitor, you have tricked me; she *is* there!"

Pate's glance had shown it; turning sharply, Severn saw before him the fearsome object that held him in a hideous bondage of hideous fear. Months, nay, it was years since his gaze had been stricken at the sight. Now as the creature stood well within the door, the already declining sun reached out a long red finger, and touched it with a blood-red impression on brow and hair.

There were now no half-lights to shadow loathsome deformity—nothing to subdue the horrible impression of the *unnatural*.

An instant Severn staggered back, while the big beads broke forth on brow and lip; then, as the figure cowered trembling to its knees, shrieking, he hurled the glass he held full at it, and, with a fearful imprecation, raised his hand to dash it down.

Then Jem Pate spoke: "Touch her, and I will kill you," he said, and Aleck Severn dropped his hand.

Jem Pate had spoken. His eyes were no longer dim as they shone into Severn's face; his feeble arms were like bands of steel as they closed round his master. He, too, was to have a moment of enthusiasm, and it had come. Severn struggled feebly a moment, then ceased resistance; the sound of the dumb man's voice rang like the voice of the dead in his ears.

"I have spilled the wine of our parting," he said; "and on *that*. Well, take it away! I dream of life, and hope, and beauty—why do you madden me with failure?"

"She longed to see your face, and I have vowed that she should," said Pate.

"Take her away," moaned Severn, shuddering and hiding his face. "She would be worse *dead*. I will not harm her; take her away!"

And, without a backward glance, the man obeyed. And so they parted, and Severn was left alone.

* * * * * * * *

It was a loneliness that would have appalled a different heart and a more wholesome imagination. As the evening drew on, the lurid sun went down behind a bank of mist, and strange sounds in the air seemed to betoken that the land was stirring in her bonds. A strong thaw-wind began to blow up from the distant sea, and by nightfall a wild gale was blowing, and the people in the little festive town made haste to take the "Christ-kind" in and shut themselves up together to laugh down in joyous, holy mirth, the eerie flapping of the great storm-wind's wings.

Outside the town gates, in that lonely cottage, the strange Christmas Eve was wearing eerily away for its solitary occupant. On every side of him were signs of flight and coming departure; on the table were still the remains of the meal as Pate had left it, and the stain of the wine marked the white paint of the door as with blood. There was no candlelight in the room, and none was needed, for either from recklessness or preoccupation the man had built up a fire of such proportions that the great stove cracked like a china teacup, and red-hot sparks and fragments of charred wood leapt out on to the polished floor. The roar of the flames was terrific—the short iron chimney glowed red hot. Was Aleck Severn awake?

His eyes were open,—wide open as if he gazed on strange sights,—but he sat like a man carved in stone. Howling and shrieking, the wind's breath caught the loosely-fastened and unshuttered casements as it passed and blew them open, but it was not the "Christ-kind" of the festival who entered on the blast.

The glare in the room shone redly out on to the snow.

Was Aleck Severn dead or living? The floor burst into flames as if the mouth of the pit had opened; columns of smoke wreathed to the ceiling; still wide open, the murderer's eyes stared before him through the fiery clouds as if he saw strange sights.

*   *   *   *   *   *   *   *

At midnight the watchman in the new "Seminary" was suddenly aroused, he knew not how. He was a bachelor and a misanthrope. Christmas to him was a season of cursed folly, and with many ominous head-shakes as to the weather, he had spent the evening in gloating gloom, and had retired before other people's fun had well begun in order to get the miserable festivity the sooner over.

He sat up in bed now, growling, his ear drums reverberating to some sound his brain had not waked quickly enough to catch.

The first thought was to look at the time, his next to grumblingly assure himself that he had been wilfully disturbed by a party of students who had had too much Schnaps; then he noticed how the gale was raging, and a certain ruddy-reflection seemed cast across his bed. "Those fellows with their torches," he snarled; then a second thought brought him to his feet with a startled bound, and, his grey hairs rising on his wrinkled brow, he rushed to the window. His trembling hand was on the blind to draw it aside, when a wild scream of hideous import rent the air and froze the old watchman's heart within him. He called on the Saints he despised to aid him, then dashed the double casements open and leaned out shouting desperately, he knew not what.

Before him stretched the snow-covered meadow, crimson-dyed, and beyond it a burning pile seemed to reach into the very clouds which, lowering and murky, scoured along before the blast, the flames reaching out greedily after them, while they glowed red with fear as they fled over the doomed place.

"Fire!" shouted the old watchman, his limbs paralysed with terror. There had been no sight like this in the town since his grandfather's days, when the wooden parish church burnt to the ground, and a priest was killed.

"Fire," he shouted again, while his gaze wandered over the illumined stretch in a dazed search for help. A shriek as of the damned answered him, and then as the loud tolling of the church bell and the rattle of the drum blown to his ears on the wind announced that the citizens had seen the fire and that succour was coming, a sight so strange burst upon the watchman's vision, that while he gazed his senses reeled, and then, not knowing whether he waked or dreamed, he fell back unconscious and prone upon the floor.

The fire aroused the whole town; in truth it was a fearful business, for the flames had attained tremendous headway. On the arrival of the crowd no living soul was to be seen or heard, and the fate of the two isolated foreigners who up to a recent day had been known to inhabit the cottage remained a terrible mystery. From the fact that absolutely no alarm had been raised, and that it was scarcely within the limits of possibility that anyone could burn to death in so small a tenement, from which egress was so easy, it was generally concluded that the inmates had abandoned the cottage before the outbreak of the fire; but their present whereabouts, if only recently fled, or the origin of the fire if the house had been long deserted, formed interesting topics of conversation among the excited townspeople watching the somewhat languid efforts of the firemen, who saw little in the empty dwelling and the flaming garden to arouse heroic deeds. The thing must burn out. Good! it was a wonderful sight while it lasted!

Meanwhile rumour and gossip flew from mouth to mouth, each version wilder than the other.

The student, Heinrich, was the originator of the most startling tales. Stimulated by the bibulous nature of the preceding evening, and half-maddened by the unusual excitement—the horrid and marvellous tolling of the bell, the rush of the wind, the roar and the glare of the flames—he had inspired a handful of emulative youths to follow at his heels while he made one dash into the burning precincts, shouting that a beautiful damsel had been concealed within the cottage, and that this was the funeral pyre of her, perchance, murdered body.

The heroic band was summarily beaten back, and the first forlorn hope was the last; but Heinrich's declamations did not cease; he yelled his tale into everyone's ears till "Schnaps" and smoke overcame him, and a paternal hand led him gently but firmly to the rear.

"Was the lad's tale true?" asked the gaping men and women. Had the two foreigners really concealed and mysteriously ill-treated a beautiful female, and was it possible that this was an incendiarism committed to hide a devilish crime? Then into their midst broke a pale and trembling figure, and shaking like an aspen leaf, covered with the thawing snow he had ploughed his way through, old Scheffel, the watchman, added the crowning wonder and horror to that memorable night.

He had seen—so he averred—two ghastly shapes break from the rear of the house as it stood in flames, and plunge into and across the meadow. They were on fire; they seemed of gigantic stature and burnt like pillars of pitch; there were two distinct screams—had no one heard them?—but no continuous cry for help. These screams were before the figures burst into sight. As they fled across the crimsoned snow the flames shot out before them, blown by the wind. It seemed to him as if one pursued the other. The sight had made him almost faint away; he described it as awful in the extreme—supernatural, Satanic.

In an appalling silence, yet moving swiftly and carrying an unearthly sound with them—so the watchman averred—the figures reached the far bank of the meadow. Here there was a moment's pause while the two flaming shapes mingled as if embracing, then the flames dying down somewhat as they ceased to move, it seemed to the paralysed watcher as if one tore the other limb from limb; but ere he could discern further, or even that fully, the darkness of a too sickening horror closed his eyes and he knew no more.

Poor old Scheffel! The candour of the tale did not bring the reward of virtue. The Committee of the Seminary being all in a body on the spot, decided that his conduct showed in a very dubious light indeed, and that watchmen who fainted at their post and were the last to arrive at the scene of a fire, had mistaken their vocation.

The crowd, full of the wildest gossip a moment before, became suddenly eminently practical. Scheffel's tale was scoffed at. If he *had* seen two wretched beings fleeing in deadly and deathly panic, he had behaved with murderous foolishness. So much of his tale was unlikely but credible. As to the ghostly silence, the gigantic stature, the tearing from limb to limb—no, no, old Scheffel had got drunk in solitary moroseness, and the sudden glare of the fire had dazzled his eyes, and in his fright he had become prophetic.

The watchman quietly accepted the rebuff and the more or less good-natured jeers, and persisted in his story. "Let them go with him to the spot in the meadow where the flaming figures had mingled as they burnt, that would prove to the unbelievers whether he told lies."

The deep snow was already slushy underfoot in the rapid thaw, and the field was dangerous and dreary to traverse, but an eager crowd, headed by the watchman himself, lost no time in taking him at his word. Skirting the now demolished dwelling, helped forward by the wind that still blew high, lighted by the sinking flames and the uncertain radiance of a boat-shaped moon, newly risen, the men and boys thronged into the meadow; as the noise and the glare died away behind them a silence fell upon the group.

Scheffel's tale began to have more weight; it seemed as if their errand might end dismally.

Presently the pioneer fell back and grasped his nearest companion's arm. "Look!" he cried, and there in the snow before them, shapeless but unmistakable, were the black prints of human feet.

At this sight anger rose in every breast against the wretched watchman; through his fatuous behaviour he had allowed two fellow creatures to perish without a hand stretched out.

"They were not human; they were devilish," muttered the old man, pushing doggedly on. "She tore him limb from limb, or he her—one was a woman,—yes, I know it. Come on."

Awed into speechlessness, they followed the tracks, more and more dismayed as they proceeded, for here and there, fallen upon the snow, were flake-like and sooty masses that stuck greasily to the touch, and smelt odiously. "Human flesh," whispered the people, and shrank together.

What had possessed these most unhappy victims to flee away *from* help? Was it, indeed, only the result of panic, or the outcome of evil passions carried to supernatural lengths?

The unuttered thought showed itself in the pale faces of the would-be rescuers as they struggled on.

As they reached the far corner of the meadow, Scheffel with a sudden access of vigour outran the rest, and stooping down over a hollow where the ground sloped away to the ditch, he uttered a loud cry, and the fictitious strength that had brought him so far suddenly failing him, he fell forward upon his knees moaning aloud.

Half afraid to look, the others crowded around. The snow in the hollow had been trampled into a black mass; in the centre was what looked like the remains of a bonfire, and of what the bonfire had been there was little room to doubt; for a single tress of a woman's long black hair streamed out from amid the hideous debris, and charred flesh and blackened bones confirmed the horrid fact that here, on a Christmas night, two creatures had burnt to death out in the open field, with ten acres of snow on either side.

But the wonder was not yet complete. The relief party, leaving the remains untouched, hastened back to the scene of the fire that was now a smoking waste, and on return-ing to the spot, accompanied by the burgomaster and the entire population, it was discovered, with a thrill of super-stitious horror, that *the long black tress of ice-wet hair was gone!*

It had been beaten into the snow, half submerged in the slush that covered the frozen depths beneath. No gale could have blown it from the place, yet it was gone.

The pious crossed themselves, and the Christmas morning dawned slowly and sadly on a pale-faced, startled crowd, the superstitious among whom pondered with many dubious shrugs and shakes as to who and what had come in with the "Christ-kind" through their gates.

So strange a story must needs fly the length and breadth of the land, but no light was ever thrown on the circum-stance. Practical people maintained that there was nothing unusual in it and that Scheffel, by his foolish panic, had left two human beings to an awful but perfectly accountable death; but with others the old man's character for veracity was fully re-established, and the eye-witness of that ghastly

Christmas episode was not allowed to regret the post of watchman, in which professional dignity would not allow the Committee to reinstate him.

The remains found in the field being, without doubt, human—though this was all that could with certainty be stated about them—they were interred with Christian ceremonies in the quaint burial ground without the town; but, in spite of the sympathy that should be naturally accorded to the victims of an awful fate, the black patch that marked where the Englishman's cottage had stood was carefully avoided, and for a time the wide meadow behind it bore an evil name, and the new watchman in the Seminary had no trouble in getting the students off the premises at night.

But in time, when the sweet young Spring had coaxed old Father Winter to let her have his Snow Princess to play with, the meadow grew too tempting a place to be let alone, and when the gorgeous flowers of summer burst into bloom behind the broken and blackened palings of the cottage-garden, children's hands could not forego the prize, and children's feet and children's laughter drove away its memories.

*   *   *   *   *   *   *   *

Another decade, and Heinrich the student had grown to manhood … and a student's life in Paris. At the little restaurant where he dined, he was wont to see, day after day, a man who interested him. The man sat for hours—his head within his hands, was incorrigibly silent, and seemed wasting with disease; but he was well-clad and paid liberally for his footing. Poverty was not his ailment. Heinrich, who remained of an investigating nature, wondered what it was. When his interest in this fellow had ripened beyond concealment, he spoke, and found the man open to acquaintanceship—to his surprise, indeed, craving sympathy. His name, he said, was Jem Pate, and he was an Englishman.

Soon after this he took to his bed, and, sitting through the long spring twilight by the dying man, Heinrich heard strange tales—stories that he half set down to the unearthly ravings of dissolution, the fantastic garblings of the parting spirit. But when Jem Pate was dead, Heinrich found upon his breast two strands of hair twisted together—one black, one gold—and he shuddered with awe and pity, and the stories that the dead man had told him became alive, and he remembered a time in his own boyhood; and his airy theories were silenced before the touch of a mystery too deep for them.

And, afterwards, in many reveries tinged with deeper and graver thoughts than had been his before, Heinrich, dwelling on the lonely inhabitant of a lonely grave, would come back to present things to feel a presence in the room and a straining as of something that would voice itself. Then he would call into the silence—"Jem Pate, is that you? Is it well with you, Jem Pate—is it well?"

FINIS.

www.ingramcontent.com/pod-product-compliance
Lightning Source LLC
Chambersburg PA
CBHW011751010726
47498CB00012B/3011